I0771249

Painted
Lies

Painted Lies, a novel

ISBN: 9798307657072

Kindle Direct Publishing
Breathe With Me, Caylin Brie
Florida, USA

Breathewithmecaylinbrie.com

Cover art by Patrick White

Printed by Kindle Direct Publishing
© 1996-2025, Amazon.com, Inc. or its affiliates.
Amazon and Kindle are trademarks of Amazon.com Inc. or its affiliates.

More by Caylin:

Sliced Time
Goldify
Change Your Story
The Human Design Guide
Human Design For Business
Human Design In Relationships
Lightworker Activation Guide
Introduction to Astrology

Dedicated to my husband, my bear, and my best friend, Patrick. Thanks for bearing with me through it all.

Introduction: Eve
All stained with blood

The paint wouldn't come out. Neither would the blood.

It had seeped into her clothes, set into her skin and was now plastered on the floor, walls, and what seemed every aspect of her existence.

Eve Brooks blinked her eyes against the darkness. The floor was hard beneath her. *There was so much blood.* She moved her arms slowly beneath her, pushing herself up, listening for the cracks of uncertainty in her body. Caked hair stuck to her face as she waited, breathed.

Drip. Drip. *Drip.*

Lights flickered to her left, making her flinch. The pipes cracked above her and she swiveled, feeling her neck strain. *Where am I?* Every noise made her heart skip. Her mind felt fuzzy, like in a dream. She slowly felt her face, her neck, desperately trying to remember. Anything.

Is this paint or blood?

The studio—warehouse style, with exposed pipes, brick walls, and plastered floor—was empty, or at least she thought. There was little to no light, so she couldn't see much. Just reflections from the tiny pools of light from the street. Streetlights. *It's nighttime.*

The blood felt like hard plaster on her knees, shins. *Dear God, it was everywhere.*

She winced as she got to her feet, her leg shooting pain right down to her toes. The lights still blinking to her left, she paused. *How long have I been here?*

Pain shot through her and her hands flew to her stomach. *Oh God.*

The floor was so cold, too cold. Her head ached with malnourishment, and her eyes closed for a minute.

Open your eyes, Eve.

Her eyes shot open.

I remember. Eve, that's my name. I'm 29 years old, I live in Del Ray, Florida, I'm an artist… her thoughts stopped there as she opened her eyes and looked around. *I remember where I am.*

The studio. *The art studio.*

Hobbling up against the wall, she attempted to stand. She forced her vision to focus, and through bloodstained tears, she saw the artwork on the walls, the floors—there it was. All hers. All stained with blood.

Chapter 1: Clay
This place

The slow drip of the water fountain was the only sound in the room. The studio had past echoes of people's laughter, but mostly it was just the energy left over from people coming and going.

Clay Burroughs wanted those people back, he wanted that energy back. He needed it to go back to normal. He was deep in thought about the studio, thinking of the years spent here. Building it. *This place.*

That was when he heard it. *Was that someone crying?*

At first he didn't know what direction it was coming from, just the sound of sobs. A deep cry, of pure pain.

No one ever really knows what to do when you hear someone crying. There is no crying protocol, only guttural instincts. And so, he tentatively walked toward the noise. Toward the girl.

"You ok?" he asked, after finding the head that was bobbing up and down in crossed arms. Red brown waves of soft hair fell over slender white shoulders.

A hard sniffle and a startled look caught in the light as her head popped up.

Eyes red with pain. Beautiful striking green eyes against a dusting of freckles.

"I—I'm sorry. I didn't think anyone was here." Her voice was small as she crossed her arms over herself protectively.

What do I say?

He looked around and pretended that it was no big deal. "Yeah, me neither."

The art studio never really had a schedule. It was organic, just like the art. People came and went, but this was a first.

Clay studied her face as she tried to calm her breathing. *I don't know how to do this.*

"You going to be alright?" He shoved his hands in his pockets because emotions with a stranger are weird.

Her face flushed a bit, perhaps realizing how embarrassing this is. She was pretty, in a raw, natural way.

She wiped at her tears and her pink stained lips tried to smile. She gathered her purse. "Yeah, totally. I'm… fine." She stammered, standing up.

He eyeballed her as she scrambled to get her things together, to get her words together. He saw her turn to leave. *Who are you?*

"I once cried to my Uber driver for an hour and my ride was only 12 minutes," he blurted out, and immediately regretted it. *It was only half true.*

The woman slowly looked up at him and cracked a slow smile.

And that was how Clay met Lyla Thurston.

Chapter 2: Eve
Why was there so much blood?

Eve pressed her hand against the blood-flecked wall and took a breath in. It hurt. *Everything hurt.*

She looked around tentatively, allowing herself a moment to see if she was safe. The noise on the street rolled on, the only light in the warehouse-style studio was the broken one flickering to her left.

"Hello?" The echo of her voice bounced back.

Nothing. Nobody seemed to care that there was blood everywhere. *No one knew yet.* She patted herself down, feeling her body for broken bones, feeling for anything. Her white dress was soaked in blood and paint.

Where is my phone?

She got to her ankle and winced. She couldn't quite see in the dark, but she felt nauseous just looking at it. So hard to tell with the blotted...*blood?*

The wall was long and she worked her way up and inched across it, every step shrieking with pain. Her leg, her hip, her foot, they all screamed in pain. She looked up at the balcony above, and zoned out into the darkness above for a moment. *Did I fall?*

Stay with it. I need to find my phone. And water.

She sucked air through her teeth and pushed off the wall, limping toward the front of the studio. As her eyes adjusted she saw it.

The room—the art—around her was destroyed, completely obliterated. The colors and compositions torn to shreds. The blood, or paint, she wasn't sure which, seemed to consume the space. Red. Everywhere. Covering the art, the hours of work, the hours of joy that her paintings brought her. Brokenness and red, everywhere.

Why was there so much blood?

There was no sign of forced entry, the sturdy, safe doors were still in tact. *I could just go right out those doors and call for help.*

She stopped though, and turned around. She was all to familiar with this place, she knew exactly where she was. And yet, she couldn't recall how she got here.

This is the art studio. But…

Wiping her nose, she dropped down into a chair she had finally reached at the front. The window was blocked by an oversized art show poster, so nobody could see in. The streets were soundless, it was dark. *What time was it?*

There was a small front desk next to her, it was bare except for a glass of half-drunk champagne, and broken bits of some type of artwork. A canvas, maybe. *My canvas.* The sudden urge to ball her eyes out welled up inside her and she let a gasp escape.

Not now.

She fought back tears and pulled at a drawer under the desk. Locked. Her head pounded with every movement. She pressed her temples and was about to lose it completely, when her right foot felt something. Soft.

Please don't be a dead body. Please don't be a dead body.

It was a small purse—a clutch. She sighed with relief. Bending down with much angst and pain, she retrieved it, opening it with red-stained fingers as quickly as she could. Red lipstick. A small bag of what she guessed was drugs, cocaine, maybe.

And a set of keys.

Chapter 3: Clay
A glimpse of Lyla

Sticking his hand out, he said, "I'm Clay. And, this is my art studio."

Technically, that was true, for now. As an artist, he felt like being a gallery owner always felt like second tier. He was an artist. But did he want to start it off with, *hi, I am a dead-end artist, struggling to make ends meet?* It had been years putting together the pieces to get to where he was today. His art studio. His art.

And now it's all being taken away from me.

She looked up and tentatively took his hand. He pulled her up slowly, allowing her to do most of the work. She nervously coughed and straightened up.

"Lyla." She was gauging whether or not he was trustworthy. He could see it. She side eyed him, looked at the door, looked back at him.

He let her name sink in to his memory. The art studio faded as he looked into her green eyes.

Her hair fell over her eye as she caught his gaze. He felt a magnetism in his blood. A chemical reaction welling up.

"This is your art studio," she said, looking around. It was as if she was just realizing where she was. She was taller than he'd expected, lean. She looked…he couldn't quite place it. *Rich.*

"Well, it was. I came to say goodbye to her, she is getting shut down." He looked around and was suddenly hit with a wave of anger, sadness, and grief, all rolled into one. *It's not fair, I put my heart and soul into this place.*

Lyla looked around, wiping her eyes one last time. "No, that can't be. This place has been around forever."

Clay changed the subject. "Listen, I just wanted to make sure you were alright. I'm not a creep or anything. You're actually…kind of, loitering," he said, with a small tilt to his lips.

"That's exactly what a creep would say." She paused, waited. "And, yes, I am loitering." She looked up, cracking her own smile.

And in the light he finally got a glimpse of Lyla.

Even with the puffy eyes and smear of mascara, she was quite breathtaking. Easy high cheeks, curly brunette bronzed waves, clothes that hugged. Her jawline showcased a full set of lips on pale skin, and his mind wandered for a moment. Magnetized.

She's definitely pretty. Striking actually.

"Well, now, I got you to smile twice since…" he trailed off, realizing he'd just made it awkward again. His hand rubbed the back of his neck.

He can see her eyeballing him in the low light, catching his features. Eyes tracing his jaw line. He ran a hand through his hair, conscious that it hadn't been cut and the tiny curls forming were unkempt. His classic looks were easy on the eyes.

Lyla paused again, not sure where to go with any of this. "I'm sorry again, for disturbing you. I don't usually cry in strange places—or with strange men." She adjusted her purse strap. Her fingers tracing the stitches down, down, down.

Clay was intrigued. *What's your story, Lyla?*

"Do you have a ride? Someplace to go?" His eyes stayed on her.

"I'll be fine. But I do hope you don't have to give this place up, I really do. I used to come here every day after work and admire the art." She gathered herself and started toward the door.

He said nothing and smiled at her, suddenly realizing he didn't want this interaction to end.

"I've already made a pretty big fool of myself for one night," she said and started backing away. "Thank you."

"Maybe if you keep coming back, I won't have to close it down," he said, in one last attempt to make this memorable. There it was, that pull again. *Don't go.*

"Maybe." She smiled and opened the door.

With a little wave, she closed it softly and was gone. Out of his life, just like that. Or so he thought.

Chapter 4: Eve
She lies

Eve's body temperature was dropping and she realized she was freezing. She rubbed her arms, feeling the hardness of cracked blood. *Or was it paint?*

She sat there, the purse in her lap, and studied the keys. *What were they to?*

Sighing, she looked around. She had to get out of here, get help, and probably get to a hospital. Yet, something was keeping her still, keeping her there; probably the pain.

Her left ankle was definitely sprained, she'd determined, and the swelling was around something she couldn't quite look at yet—in the darkness it was too hard to tell. She felt like her insides were bruised. Those were only some of the internal injuries she calculated—on the outside, she was one big bruise, scrapes up and down her legs and arms, like shards. She grabbed her stomach again.

Did I fall through glass?

Behind her, she felt for the wall, searching for a light fixture, a lamp, a plug, anything. Slowly, her fingers found a switch. She flicked it on, hoping against hope that it would work.

The lights flared above her in a harsh buzz. Electric lighting above her shocked her eyes and she shielded them for a second. Until she saw the massacre. *Oh no.*

She slowly turned and looked out—it was a battlefield of broken artwork, everywhere. Canvasses were broken, smashed, shattered. The walls were covered in red paint, or blood—or a mixture.

Her hand flew to her mouth as she assessed the damage. Taking it all in, she saw bits and pieces of her time, energy, creativity, torn into smithereens. She saw sprays of crimson red everywhere, covering ever piece of art that still hung, haphazardly on walls, splattered. This was devastation, in art form.

She shuddered. *Why?*

Her mind was blank. The purse in her lap fell to the floor, as she saw the podiums of art that were tipped over, red paint, or blood, smeared over them crudely. Across from her on the wall, written in blood red, were the words —

SHE LIES.

Chapter 5: Clay
The walls will be bare soon

Two days went by, and there hadn't been a moment where Clay didn't think of her face in the shadow, her eyes filled with tears. *Why hadn't I asked her to stay?*

He wiped his forehead, sweat dripping slowly down as he stopped gripping the hammer so tight. He had taken his shirt off as the studio was stifling, the air had been cut off a week ago. The ladder whined beneath him, as if it was tired. A nail had just dropped, again.

Sighing, he dropped down, rung by rung to the floor, looking for the lost nail. *This place.* This place that had caused him so much anguish, but brought him so much joy.

The studio. *My studio.*

He remembered when it became his. It was serendipity, for sure, but it belonged to him. It always had. This corner studio, with the one tiny window, the studded brick walls, the space to see art come alive, it called him in.

Every time he passed it on the street, he saw himself there—not the center of attention, not even the artist, just the one who allowed others to showcase their art, their soul.

His art was complicated. Sculptures of his past. Bits and pieces of people's faces, memories. Larger than life sculpted memories.

To see it slip away was killing him. But what could he do? The money slipped away with it, and so did the art. People would always want art, or so he'd thought. He was on his own and the money just wasn't there. The bills were.

But with digital images, the dawn of AI, and the unfolding of the American dream… there it was. The last on the list of things to do for just about anyone. Art.

But not Lyla.

Her face glimmered in his mind for a minute. She had said she came there every day. He frowned, except today. *If she came here every day…why wouldn't others?*

The signs were there, for sure. The signs to hold on, to hold out. Don't close just yet, there could be hope. But the bills kept coming, and the people did not. So, the decision was made. Or so he thought.

A small rap on the door intruded his thoughts. His hair fell in his eye as he swung his face toward the window, hope rushing to his chest.

Lyla.

A bird. A tapping beak against glass. Wind gust, and the bird was gone.

Not Lyla. Idiot, stop thinking about her.

He climbed the ladder once more, steadying it against the wall and heaving his body up the steps. The walls will be bare soon and he will have to move on.

Move on, Clay.

The ladder shifted under his weight again as he heard another rap, at the window this time. *Damn, bird. That's it. Just get the job done, and get out of here.*

He pulled the nail out of the wall, desperately trying to hang onto it with the hammer, and hold the ladder at the same time. He sighed out heavily as the nail slipped through again and fell to the floor. He cursed loudly, hearing his voice echo in the silent warehouse.

Rapping again at the window. He turned around at the top of the ladder, startled this time, by how loud it was.

And, there she was.

Chapter 6: Eve
A small protruding bone

Stifling her tears, Eve grabbed the keys out of the purse, and tried to stand tall. Well, first she just tried to stand.

Ow. Ow, ow, ow.

Slowly making her way through broken glass, sticky champagne, and blood-paint, she started her way to the back of the studio.

*The storage closet, the bathrooms, the office…*her mind was replaying what was all back there. *Was there a back door?*

She suddenly didn't want anyone to see this bloody massacre, it somehow felt like it would all be pinned on her. She knew she didn't do this…*did I?* Her mind reeled as she slow shuffled her way to the back.

She stopped. *Should I turn the lights off?*

Yes, her mind said, slowly. Don't draw attention right now. She huffed and slowly pushed back to the light switch.

Eyeballing the streets outside as best she could through the poster-sized advertisement, she saw nothing.

The darkness enveloped her, and her eyes adjusted. The slow glow off the streetlamp seeped in and she was able to meander through the rubble. Hobbling through it all, she let out a whimper in pain.

The door to the back room was closed, of course, it always was. The light was so dim, but she pulled the set of keys out and eyed them. They looked small. Of course the first key didn't work. Then, when the second key didn't work she slammed her fist in frustration on the door and the hinge popped. *It was open this whole time?*

She cursed under her breath, feeling like an idiot for not just trying the knob first. Then she swung the door open slowly, leaning on the doorway for support. Her breath was uneven, her heart rate elevating.

Is someone in here? Still trying to kill me?

She pushed the door all the way open and allowed the shallow room to lift in the shadows. She felt along the wall for a switch and flipped it on, holding her breath.

A small lamp in the far corner of the room lit up, and she froze as she saw that it was all in order.

The sofa, desk, lamp, chairs, even the bathroom across the way—all in perfect order.

No one's here.

She inched her way in and shut the door behind her slowly. This place felt familiar. *I need to think.* She looked around and immediately headed for the door across the room—the bathroom, *finally.*

When she hit the tile floor, her foot cried out and she slammed into the sink. Turning the water on she cupped it and drank greedily. *So thirsty.*

The small shrouded mirror in the dim light was poor, but she could see herself. Her sun bleached hair was caked in streaks, packed with bloody paint and pressed against her scalp. One long streak of red went from her face to her neck, like a lash from a whip. Her cheek was badly bruised, and it was puffing her left eye up, where there were broken blood vessels shouting at her. Her dress was ripped, shredded in parts, where bits of glass lay embedded, like they were part of the fabric.

And, there was a small bone protruding from her ankle.

My God.

And that's when it went dark for Eve Brooks.

Chapter 7: Clay
Angel investor

Clay watched as Lyla cupped the window, looking inside. Her auburn hair billowed in the breeze. He watched, surprise filling his chest. *Lyla.*

Her eyes landed on him—shirtless, sweating—and she breathed out, fogging the window a bit. She watched as he climbed down the ladder, wiping his hands on his pants slowly.

He thought he could see a smile curl at her lips. He walked up to the door and pushed it out towards her. His heart skipped a pace, that magnet feeling taking over. *Steady now.*

"Hi," he said, leaning on the doorway.

Lyla stepped back and took him in for a moment. He was a work of art himself. He was sculpted out of muscle, taut skin, tanned and fit. His sandy blonde hair tousled from the ocean breeze, a few strands falling carelessly over his forehead. His sun-kissed skin, still warm from hours spent on the beach, gave him that effortless, surfer-handsome vibe, like he'd stepped straight out of the waves and into the world with little effort.

His easy smile and relaxed demeanor made him the kind of guy who seemed like he belonged wherever the sun was shining, effortlessly capturing attention without ever trying too hard. He smiled and she saw a dimple emerge, his sandy blonde hair softly falling forward as he leaned out. His jeans hugged at his hips, worn and torn with use.

"Hey."

"Come on in." He eyed the street, the palm trees swaying a bit, the couples walking, the balmy breeze flowing through. He took a deep breath of salty air.

"Thanks." She stepped in and to the left squarely.

He was conscious of how close she was, and that he did not have a shirt on. Closing the door gently, he looked at her with a smile. "You missed a day."

She sniffed a laugh and said, "I wanted to say thanks…" she trailed off, looking around.

"It's nothing. You were just trespassing," he said, the smile returning.

She smiled again, showing straight, expensive teeth. "I also wanted to tell you that you're not giving up on this place."

He lifted his eyebrows, surprised. *Where is this going?*

She continued. "I'm going to buy it. Consider it my… help." She was walking around, sizing it up. Her piercing green eyes had plans.

"You want to buy it?" He was genuinely curious now, crossing his arms over his chest.

"I have…funds. It's a long story but I want to put it toward something *good*. Something meaningful. I'm officially investing in Burroughs Art Studio. You can think of me as your angel investor—and you can still run the place." She squared her shoulders.

"Angel investor," he repeated. *Is she serious?*

"Yes. You see, that's why I was crying. Well, it was one of the reasons, anyway. My parents just died… they were, well, they died." She stopped and turned away, masking something. "They left me with more than enough to help you."

He softened. "I'm sorry."

"You may have known them. Carol and Vincent Thurston." She looked back at him, waiting for recognition. Her eyes searched his.

No way.

"Your parents were Vincent and Carol Thurston?"
Clay asked, his eyes widening. *I've definitely heard of
them.*

Vincent and Carol Thurston were multi-billionaires
out of Miami, and owned hundreds of media agencies
in the southeast area. As CEOs of Thurston Media
Group, they'd built an empire by turning journalism
into a lucrative machine. Their innovation wasn't just
in creating content—it was in monetizing the very
labor of the reporters and writers who fueled it. By
exploiting the rise of digital platforms, they
developed sophisticated models that transformed
journalistic work into a high-revenue stream.
Reporters were paid pennies per click, while Vincent
and Carol amassed billions through ads, syndications,
and data analytics. In the media world, they were
celebrated as visionaries; but to critics, they were
ruthless moguls who had profited from the labor of
others, all while shifting the media landscape in ways
that reshaped the very definition of truth.

They had been making money off of media agencies,
journalists, and big hitters…you name it, for decades.

"Yes, *them,*" she said uncomfortably, like she had
just revealed a secret.
"Anyway, they're…gone. And, they left me, well they
left me a lot. And what I want to invest in…is you."
She sighed, as if she had gotten it all out. Her face
tightened.

He opened his mouth to respond, but as soon as he did, the lights went out and they were both left standing there, in the dark.

Shit.

Chapter 8: Eve
Footsteps

The wet tile floor was what Eve tasted when she woke up. Her cheek was against the cold, dirty tile and she was in pain. *So much pain.*

Pushing herself up, she grabbed her ankle and cried out. Now her head hurt too, and she didn't know which to grab first. *Did I faint?*

The bathroom around her was small and a buzzing light overhead was horribly annoying. She felt her head, a small bump yes, right under her chin, she must have hit the sink on the way down. Just adding injuries on injuries, now.

I'm okay, I'm okay, she tried to reassure herself, and winced.

She sat back, and closed her eyes. She felt the bump on her head and it reminded her of a similar one years ago. Memories flooded her vision. She closed her eyes, and for a moment, the sunshine and palm trees faded away, replaced by the memory of that cold night in Michigan. The sharp sting of betrayal had felt like a punch to the gut when she found out about him, the man she had loved, seeing someone else behind her back. She had never imagined he'd be capable of such a thing, but there it was, the truth laid bare. It was the breaking point—that fight—and she needed to escape. That's why she had packed up and moved to Florida, away from the life she thought she'd had, away from the pain of knowing she'd been replaced. She had come here to heal, to start over, but the past was never far behind. Neither were the bruises. And now this.

Stop. Just stop.

She sat up straight and looked around, trying to brush the past off. Pushing herself up, she hoisted herself on the toilet, and then immediately had to urinate.

Sighing, she pushed her now painted dress up, pulling the thin panties down, so she could go. She breathed in, tears welling up.

Don't, Eve. Not now.

That was when she heard a sound.

What was that? She stopped breathing completely, and listened as hard as she could. There it was again.

Footsteps.

Chapter 9: Clay
The breaker box

Lyla reached out for Clay, in the dark. Her hands wrapped around his shoulder and she pulled him in. He hesitated, listening.

She pulled in even closer, circling her arms around his waist, like a coiling snake.

They both stood there, the silence growing. Their hearts beating, waiting.

"Hello?" Clay's voice was gruff, as he called out. He pulled away from Lyla's touch. *Why did she just do that?*

"The breaker probably. It's in the back, but there is stuff everywhere. Follow me." His heart thudded as tried to focus in the dark.

Did I lock the door?

Lyla's skin was hot as she followed him. They inched along, foot by foot, sliding through the darkness to the back. They only bumped into one thing—that damn ladder—and then found their way to the back office.

"The breaker box…is around here, somewhere." He felt the walls, felt the molding. She followed, her hand now on his waist.

He felt goosebumps at her touch. There it was again, that pull.

Lyla waited until they stopped, and before Clay knew what was happening, she slowly turned his hips around so he faced her. *What is she doing?*

She traced her fingers up his chest and to his mouth, pulled up on her tiptoes, and kissed him. Softly.

Clay froze, paused for a moment. Then softly, slowly, kissed her back. *What am I doing?*

Time stood still for eons, and that magnetic pull felt powerful as they locked lips and arms. It was only when his elbow bumped the shiny metal of the breaker box door, that they broke the spell.
Unsure if he should leave this moment, he smiled down at her and turned around.

He flicked a switch with a triumphant breath out. Lyla released her grip as the lights turned on around them. Her hands were hot.

He looked at her, smiled, half-concerned. "You good? Sorry, I told you this place was shutting down. They're trying to get rid of me." He looked down, away. *What do I do now?*

She paused and looked around. His stuff was still everywhere. He had boxes that were open, empty, filled. She turned around slowly, taking it in.

"This is not happening." She turned straight to him. "We're going to save this place," she said, her pose changing a bit, straightening. "Today."

"Today?" He laughed softly. *She's insane.*

"You don't have much of a choice. I'm here, serendipitously, and I am throwing money at you to fix this. And you're helping me by taking this investment on—financially." She paused.

His smile was widening. He stood there, hands on hips, and smiled even bigger. *This is going to be a bad idea.*

"I'm in."

Chapter 10: Eve
They were in here

"Hello?"

Eve heard the far off voice and her blood pulsed in her ears as she held her breath. She slowly reached over and turned the light off, the bathroom door slightly ajar.

And she waited.

She could hear them getting closer now, the footsteps. They were now walking through the war of art out there. The words flashed before her eyes.

SHE LIES.

"Hello?" The voice again, deep, a man's voice. A familiar voice.

Eve watched through the slice of light as the office door was pushed open. A flashlight beam hit the floor and turned off when the lamp filled the room. The end of a gun turned the corner first. Then one foot, then an arm, then another.

They were in here. She pressed her eyes shut and waited. The footsteps got closer.
Her breath held, she was gripping the toilet seat with both hands, her leg pounding with pain. The tall figure moved through the small slit of bathroom door.

This is it. This is where I die.

And to her total cliche disbelief, her whole life flashed through her mind then. She saw herself growing up on the lake, the smell of rain. She heard her mother's laugh, saw her father's face. She felt the rush of memories flood her mind as if she were standing at the edge of a lake right now, watching the waves lap in endless succession, each one carrying fragments of her past.

She felt her childhood in Michigan—a life spent chasing fireflies on warm summer nights, her bare feet pressing into soft, cool grass, and the laughter of her family echoing around the lake house.

She thought of her parents, their steady love and quiet strength, with whom she'd shared secrets and fights, and the pets that had come and gone, each one a chapter of comfort or heartbreak.

The years blurred so fast, faces of old loves and exes flickered like fading photographs—some sweet, some bitter.

Faces of friends who'd faded from her life, the ones who had slipped through her grasp without warning, now hovered just beyond her reach, and with them, the realization that time had passed, irretrievable and relentless. She felt ashamed she hadn't amounted to much, just an artist who fled home with a broken heart. She hadn't accomplished her life goals, her purpose. Not yet.

All of this happened in the span of a few seconds. The lights shifted, and she snapped her eyes open, as the figure moved around the room, searching. She listened as the footsteps got closer.

Daring a breath, she waited.

The noise stopped and the footsteps made their way slowly to the door. The door pushed open and the light peeked in. And, with the flick of a switch, she was caught in the harsh light, and instinctively her hands flew up. She blinked furiously.

Don't kill me.

"D-don't hurt me," she stammered, her eyes still adjusting. They were wet and smeared with red blood and paint, and she was having trouble focusing.

Please don't kill me.

"Evie?" The voice dropped, along with the gun.

She stared out, eyes wide and froze.

"Dalton?"

Chapter 11: Clay
Let things be okay

The next day, rain was pelting the windows. The storm had been going for hours. Clay wiped his hands on his pants, this time, in a very different way than yesterday. It was in excitement, hope.

The boxes were coming back out. The ladder was put away. The lights were back on. Things were going to be okay.

Please let things be okay.

He looked around, in disbelief. The call had come through that morning. The papers were signed, the money was in the right accounts, the studio was back in business. *How did it happen so fast?*

It all seemed so surreal. As he placed the sign back up in the window, he paused. *Open.*

He took a breath and let it sink in. The art studio would remain open. And then fear gripped his heart because he realized it. *I need to keep it open.*

Lyla flashed across his mind.

He could feel her against him, in the dark, scared but strong. He remembered how she felt, it like she was off limits.

Suddenly caught with a wave of guilt, he stopped himself. *Jamie.*

It had been three years since his wife Jamie's passing, and yet, there were days when it still felt like a fresh wound, as though he could still hear her laughter echoing in the corners of the studio, feel her warm touch on his arm. She had been his everything—the one person who understood him completely. But as he sat there now, he realized something had shifted. The grief that had once consumed him, relentless and overwhelming, had slowly begun to fade, replaced by something quieter, more peaceful. He still missed her —he always would—but he no longer felt trapped by the pain. He was ready to move on. Maybe not to forget, but to let the memory of Jamie become a part of the past, no longer a shadow hanging over him, but a light that would always guide him forward.

The thoughts stirred him, but the grief had settled. Time never resolves grief completely, but it does soften the blow. He was ready to share his life with someone, build a family even, maybe. Who knows. He just knew he was ready to share the rest of his time here with someone.

The palm trees brushed against the window, the storm getting heavier. Rain came pushing against the studio. He came back to this moment and frowned at the storm. He needed people to come through that door. Stat.

The door swung open then, and he was pulled from his thoughts. The rain blew in, and the light shifted. He saw two figures enter the studio, windblown and laughing.

That was fast.

"Hello?" He squinted. Looking out from the back, the studio seeming so big just then.

"Hey, Clay." A familiar voice. Her voice.

"Lyla?" He got up and saw her, standing there, close to a man. Very close.

"We wanted to come by and congratulate you." Her eyes darted back and forth between the two men. Looking at Clay, she cleared her throat.

We.

"This is Dalton Price, my fiancé."

Chapter 12: Eve
There it was, the finger

Dalton's gun shook a bit as he stared down at her. "Evie, is that you?"

Eve let out a big breath, and shuddered. Her shoulders sagged with relief and she said his name again softly, "Dalton."

He softened, and holstered his gun. Rushing to her, he knelt down. His dark, tousled hair always seemed to be just a little out of place, he had the rugged look of someone who spent more time on the streets than in a neatly pressed uniform. His broad shoulders and muscular build were the result of years of physical training, but it wasn't just his strength. There was something in the way he carried himself—calm, focused, like he was always prepared for whatever the next moment might throw at him.

His dark eyes, sharp and calculating, missed nothing, scanning the room with the precision of a seasoned cop. Every inch of him, from the faint stubble on his chin to the way he moved, spoke of a man who had seen too much, but was still standing strong.

Eve's eyes focused.

Dalton stood leaning over her, his tall frame cutting through the bathroom light with easy confidence. His sharp features—high cheekbones and a jawline that seemed to be chiseled from stone—all staring down at her intently.

She relaxed. *Dalton. He looked good.*

"Are you…okay?" he asked, assessing the damage. He scanned her face, her arms, looking her up and down, and landed on her ankle. "You need a hospital."

"Yeah," she managed. Pain shot through her core and she grabbed her stomach, again. *No.* "Thank God you're here," she mumbled, feeling the exhaustion hit her.

"We need to get you to a hospital—*now*," he said, looking around. His eyes were concerned. "What the hell happened here?"

"I-I really don't know." She rubbed at her head, trying to will the information to come to her. All she felt was bloody paint.

"You don't remember?" he asked, examining her head, searching for recognition in her face. He slowly poked at the blood-streaked strands of her hair.

She tried to raise her head, to shake it, but she was too tired. The injuries and pain were taking over and she was fading fast.

"Dalton…" she stopped, looking at him.

Eve remembered her relationship with Dalton vividly. Too vividly. She remembered the fight mostly. It had escalated so quickly—words spoken in anger, insults flying, both of them pushing each other's buttons until everything spiraled out of control. He hadn't mean to hurt her, but in the heat of the moment, he had grabbed her too roughly, his hands coming down hard on her shoulder as she tried to push past him. The instant she flinched, his heart shattered. He had never seemed like the kind of man who'd hurt anyone, especially her—the one person he'd promised to protect. But in that moment, he saw the fear in her eyes, and the weight of his actions crushed him. He wanted to apologize, to take it all back, but the damage was done, and he knew it was too late. She could remember all of these moments, but she couldn't remember last night.

She stopped the mad swirl of memories. *Wait. why was Dalton even here?*

She was about to ask and the room fuzzed before her. She shifted, looking at him from the side. His gaze had not faltered, he sat, prone, waiting for her to speak.

"Why…" she started.

He blinked, and she caught the hesitation. She felt the energy in the room shift as he prepared his answer.

He knows something. *SHE LIES.*

"Let's get you some help." He slowly lifted her off the toilet and positioned her in his arms. The leg hung and she shrieked out in pain as he hoisted her up. "We can talk about everything later." His words were getting further and further away.

She smelled him, that familiar smell. The bathroom tiles felt so far away. Her head bobbed on his shoulder, as she passed the office, the lamp, the desk. Her vision started to blur as the studio lights hit her, and then she saw it.

The finger.

"Dalton!" she shouted, startling him as he walked. "A finger. A finger! There, there, *there,*" she stammered, pointing wildly toward the corner.

Dalton turned, and there it was. A human bloody finger.

Chapter 13: Clay
I'm definitely interested

Dalton extended his hand out to Clay, smiling genuinely. "Hi, nice to meet you," he said casually, as if he was invited.

Clay wiped his hands on his pants, yet again, and cleared his throat. The two men exchanged a strong handshake, perhaps a bit too strong.

"Clay." His voice was even. *Fiancé, huh?*

Lyla backed up a bit from both of them. Pausing, she eyed Clay, gauging his anger. "I didn't even get a chance to tell you, but…you helped me realize some things. That my investments are important. Investments like Dalton."

Clay didn't say anything, just nodded, slowly. *You kissed me and you're with this guy?*

Clay regained composure. "I thought you'd mentioned there were two things you were crying about. This must be the other thing," he said, fully aware that he had just insulted Dalton.

Lyla's cheeks tinted slightly and she turned around, looking at the space around her.

"And this is Clay's studio—well, *our* studio," she said, winking at him.

Clay suddenly felt stifled. He eyed Lyla, and defensive thoughts raced through his mind at once. *You don't own me, Lyla.*

Lyla's eyes were dark with red rims as she held his stare. She broke eye contact and turned around slowly in circles. "It's going to be so great. Just wait and see." She ran her finger along the desk top.

Dalton slowly wandered away, with his hands tucked behind his back, looking at random pieces of artwork.

Clay and Lyla stood in the studio silence for a moment. "You failed to mention the second thing," Clay said, squaring Lyla right in the eye.

"I know. I wasn't sure it was going to work out until this morning. I didn't want to overcomplicate things," she responded, but her eyes said differently.

He nodded, his lips tight. "Okay, Lyla."

"Nothing changes between us," she said, her fingers trailing the edge of the table between them.

Dalton walked back and clapped his hands on Lyla's shoulders, making her jump slightly. She moved out from under his grasp, looking around. He leaned on the desk, observing her. A gun poked out behind Dalton's jacket and Clay caught it. *You're a cop?*

Dalton rested his hands on his hips. "Nice place. My ex—my *friend*," he corrected, "might want to showcase her art here. If you're interested."

Lyla and Dalton exchanged glances.

Clay took his time answering, then slowly nodded, not taking his eyes off of Lyla.

"Yes, I'm definitely interested."

Chapter 14: Eve
He's hiding something

Eve rubbed her stomach, mindlessly. It had been hours in the hospital bed since she woke up.

The sterile scent of antiseptic hung in the air, mingling with the faint hum of machines nearby. Her head felt heavy, as if someone had placed a weight on top of it, and her body was wrapped in a strange kind of stillness—both distant and aware. She blinked, trying to focus on the room around her. The walls were a pale, neutral shade, lined with machines and monitors, their blinking lights offering a strange comfort, like quiet sentinels watching over her.

Somewhere in the distance, the sound of nurses' footsteps echoed in the hall. She swallowed, her throat dry, and tried to sit up, only to be stopped by a dull ache that spread from her abdomen. It was then that she realized—she wasn't sure exactly what had happened, but something had changed.

She was told that Dalton rushed her to the hospital, called the police, and then she was sent off to surgery for her ankle. They were reviewing her diagnostics.

A rush of air through the door interrupted her thoughts. Dalton flashed his badge to the nurse just outside as he made his way into the room.

She groggily looked up, sunk in the bed. *Always flashing his badge.* "Hey," she seeped out, her throat coarse.

"You're up," he said and handed her a cup of lukewarm water. He sat at the edge of the bed. "How's the ankle?"

She sipped the water slowly. "Numb. I actually don't even know."

"That tracks. With what you told me, you don't know much," he stated.

Always a cop. She groaned a bit, not interested in reliving the horror that she just endured. And now, she was here, with no information, no phone, no idea what had happened. It flooded back and tears pooled at her eyes.

"Hey, we're going to figure this out," he said, placing a hand over hers. She instinctively pulled it back slightly.

That was when she remembered. *The finger.*

"Did you find out who's finger it was?"

Her words stopped him and he looked up sharply.

"It's being processed right now, we don't know anything yet. We should have some information soon. Don't worry about that right now."

"Don't worry? This is all directed at me, did you forget?" She pushed herself up in the bed, feeling her face get hot. *No one wants to know more than me.*

"We'll know something soon."

Eve sighed, seeing how intense this was for him too. She didn't want to be reminded of her past with Dalton.

"I want to know the second you find something— okay? I want to know who did this. They're still out there." *They're still out there trying to kill me.*

He nodded.

"And the keys? The set I found, did you find anything?" Her thoughts were coming back now. Her mind a bit clearer.

His eyes trailed back to her, and there was a glint. Again, a hesitation.

"What is it?" *He knows something.*

"We believe they're to a safety deposit box. We haven't located which one yet." He looked at her, and collected himself.
Eve sighed and rubbed her head.

"You will be the first to know, for both, I promise. Just rest for now." He started to get up, but she grabbed his arm.

Eve's mind blurred. Visions of him leaning in to kiss her pressed into her memories. *Stop.*

Dalton's eyes registered as if he knew what she was thinking.

"Regardless of what happened between us in the past, please just do me a solid and help me find out who did this?" Her voice was steadier now, pleading.

He nodded again and left. The door closed softly.

He's hiding something.

Chapter 15: Clay
No more questions

The days flipped by on the calendar. Clay tried to think—two had gone by, maybe three. The palm trees swayed in the breeze outside, just like always. The studio came to life, as promised.

Clay stood now, looking at the studio walls, complete. It was officially done, and he leaned on his mop, admiring his work. The walls were filled with art, the podiums were set, the floors were cleaned, he was ready.

He sighed. *Why don't I feel ready?*

Together, with his brother's help, he had brought it back to life. *Well, along with Lyla's money.* He clenched his jaw, and leaned the broom in the corner.

His brother—Patrick, married, two kids, two car garage, walk-in closet—had grilled him hard, asking a lot of questions. Without saying too much, Clay told him he had just gotten lucky. He dodged the questions of who she was, and why she wanted to invest. Patrick knew something was up but didn't press it. He'd left with a firm handshake and a look that said, you'll tell me everything later.

Clay was just happy Patrick was around again. Their bond had not always been there but had deepened in ways neither had anticipated after the loss of Jamie and their father in the same year. Grief became something they shared in the silence between words, in the long nights spent talking about their memories, fears, and regrets. Patrick, always the stoic one, found himself leaning on Clay more than he ever had before, while Clay, who had often felt overshadowed by his older brother, discovered a new depth of strength in his own heart.

Together, they navigated that fragile line between mourning and healing, realizing that the weight of their shared sorrow could either tear them apart or help them be closer. And in the end, it was the latter.

Clay didn't feel lucky right now, though. He felt right back where he was before all of this. At the beginning of it all—starting over, again.

A phone vibrated somewhere and interrupted his thoughts. He patted his pockets. His cell phone was in the office. He turned on his heel and started toward the back, when he realized the front door had just opened.

The phone stopped ringing, he'd missed it. *Great.*

He heard the crying, then.

There is no way that I'm hearing that cry, again.

The door slammed shut against the breeze, and warm air blew in. The studio shifted and Lyla rushed in. He blinked in the light.

She ran right in, throwing her purse down on the desk and whirling around to him. Her sobs were going strong as she rushed past the desk, and right into Clay's arms. He took a step back as she leaned into him, pressing her face into his chest, the tears still coming.

"Lyla, what's wrong?" His voice was calm but he was lighting up all over. *What had he done? If he hurt her…*

Clay's head rested on hers as she calmed her breathing. He could feel her softening against him, as her shudders slowed to a halt.

"I'm sorry. I…" Lyla's voice was small, shadowed against his shoulder. She wiped her eyes and pulled away, but not far. With his arms still around her, he waited.

She looked up at him, her face was shiny with tears. Her striking green eyes vibrated with energy, scanning his face. He could see her wrestling with something below the surface.

Even sad, I'm pulled to you.

He reached up and moved a stray hair out of her eyes, still holding her. "This is the second time you've been in my arms this month."

Before he knew it, her lips were on his and pressing, hard. She was on tiptoes unfolding into him, and allowing the kiss to happen, fully.

He was surprised, eyebrows up, but only for a split second.

What am I doing?

He scooped her up and kicked the door shut behind him. Setting her down gingerly on the desk, he kissed her. He was consumed by her suddenly, like he was under a spell. *Lyla.*

Words were trying to escape her mouth, but all that came out were moans. He kissed her cheeks, her jaw, her neck. She grabbed at his back and shoulders, trying to get closer to him even though she was practically one with him.

No, we can't do this.

He stopped, pushed her off gently, and looked at her. But she just kept barreling forward.

She took his shirt up over his head, and met him back at his lips.

He tried pulling back and again she pulled him in.

"Lyla, no. This is wrong." *This is wrong.*

And then he saw it, on her shoulder blade. A scar running from her neck down her spine in a jagged, ripped line. Red skin pulled at the edges of it.

"What happened here?" he asked tentatively between breaths. *What did he do to you?*

She said nothing, and kissed him even harder. Grabbing at him forcefully, she pulled him off the desk and pushed him onto the sofa. She mounted him and took what she wanted.

No more questions.

Chapter 16: Eve
His hands on her

Eve's eyes shot open. *Where am I?*

It was late, the hospital lights were off. She could hear a low beeping out in the hall. Then it set in. She was still in the hospital but being dismissed tomorrow, and sent to physical therapy for the ankle. All injuries were healing, slowly, but no permanent internal damage. The doctors had said her memory would come back, to just give it time.

I should feel grateful.

But she didn't feel grateful. She felt vengeful. She felt obsessed. Thoughts were swirling as her mind was putting pieces together. She could remember everything in her life, all major events, people, places, her life story…she could remember it all. And, yet couldn't remember that night. She closed her eyes again, trying desperately to remember. She tried to walk back in her memory, before that night. It felt like a dream, wisps of memories floating in and out. But one question remained.

Who would do this to me?

She sighed. The worst part was, she didn't have her phone. Her parents were states away. She was alone in this hot, balmy town, and hated herself for even trying to find a new place to call home. She'd been here for months and Dalton was the only person she'd met. Maybe she should just go back home to Michigan.

Was Dalton the only person I'd met?

That felt wrong rolling around in her brain. She looked up. The night nurse was nowhere to be found, and Eve was feeling restless. She needed to move her body, move this energy. *I need to remember.*

She struggled to get up, knowing that she would need to get used to the crutches. Grumbling as she reached for them, she slid off the bed.

As she touched her foot down, it felt better than the other day. She sighed and hobbled up and to the doorway. The hallway was dim, small night lights lining the walls casting an upward shadow. Machines on either side of her along the walls were slowly, monotonously beeping and flickering with lights.

As she walked the hallway, she felt like a mental patient. Going over that night again and again in her head.

SHE LIES.

What did it mean? She tried to remember that night. The art show. Her art show. It had been a dream come true for her, from what she remembered. Her art came together at the last minute, everything fell into place. She remembered…yes…painting those big pieces. *Yes, it's coming back. My spirit animals.*

She remembered, it was a series of large animal prints, up close images of animals' eyes, alluring and exotic, filled with intrigue—she thought so anyways. She was proud of it—all of it. There was catered food, champagne, and music. She closed her eyes for a minute imagining the broken glasses of champagne all over the floor.

SHE LIES.

She shook her head, and shuffled on. She forced herself to remember the studio. She recalled being up on a balcony looking down over the show, feeling proud. She had worked hard to get to this point. She was…happy. Getting a gallery showcase was a pretty big deal as an artist. The gallery, the art studio. But she was happy because of something else. She got a flash of a face, a man. *A handsome man.*

She pressed her eyes shut trying to remember. Her crutch hit the linoleum, and squished alongside her. Her foot dragged a bit, and the hallway droned on.

Come on, Eve, remember.

Then she saw it. Or more felt it. Eve stood before the canvas, the colors swirling in her mind like a puzzle she couldn't quite solve. The strokes were familiar, yet foreign—something deep inside her knew this was her work, but she couldn't place the connection. A man's voice echoed in her ears, gentle yet insistent, describing the first time he saw her art, how it took his breath away.

Her mind flashed, bright smile, curl to the hair. His hands on her.

Clay.

Chapter 17: Clay
Should not have done that

The hard cushion of the sofa pricked at Clay's skin. The musty office smelled like bad choices and dust. He blinked his eyes open and looked around at the room. He whirled around on the sofa, and saw nothing. No Lyla. *Ugh.*

His reality hit him then—last night. *With her.*

His head dropped and he pushed his legs over the edge of the cushion. He sighed out a breath and made his way to the bathroom.

The light filled the small room and his mind couldn't help but go over what happened. Looking himself in the mirror, he felt guilt. Shame. *It was wrong.*

He came out of the bathroom and turned the lamp on, looking for his phone. There were two messages. One from his brother and one from an unknown number. He opened his voicemail and patiently waited while he listened to Patrick's request to call him back.

Then, the second voice crackled in on the other end.

"Hi. This is Eve Brooks and I'm interested in learning more about your art studio. I'm…an artist and would like to find out more…information." The voice was breezy and the wind caught the phone line. He listened intently. "Anyway, please give me a call back at this number, and thank you, in advance. I love your studio."

Clay listened one more time, not because he wasn't paying attention, but to hear her voice. *She loves my studio.*

He shook his head and dialed the number back. No answer. He left a voicemail, and told her to come by the studio any time and he would get her that information. He lingered before saying anything else, and then quickly hung up. Hope sprung to his chest. Then sunk again when he thought about last night.

What am I going to do about Lyla?

The day moved forward and so did his thoughts. The room reminded him of last night, as he tried to work. He sighed, and allowed the thought to come through that he was fighting to come to terms with. *Should not have done that.*

He needed to go up to his apartment, to freshen up. He'd felt like he'd been living down here in the studio.

He grabbed his phone and began to head out. The studio could wait an hour.

The light peeked into the windows as he made his way across the warehouse floor. He stopped for a minute, admiring his work. He had brought it back.

Well, Lyla brought it back.

Not only that, but there was a hunk of clay that had been delivered yesterday, just waiting for him on the large wood art table—just waiting for him to begin sculpting. All he had to do was start. The pile on the parchment paper begged him.

Why was it so hard to start?

He was just turning on his heel, grabbing his keys, when there was a small, faint knock at the front door.

Lyla.

He picked up his pace and went to the door, it was unlocked. *Of course it was, because she left so early.*

He swung the heavy door open, flooding himself with light so bright he squinted.

"Hi," a soft voice said against the breeze.

Hair blew in all directions around her face, sunglasses glinting in the light. Her golden blonde waves, damp from the sea breeze, cascaded in soft tendrils around her shoulders, catching the light like strands of sun. A cool saltiness clung to her skin. Her sun-kissed face glowed with a natural beauty, a hint of freckles across her nose, and her eyes—vibrant and warm—held a quiet confidence.

She smiled, a flash of something playful in the curve of her lips, and for a heartbeat, Clay wasn't sure if he was more struck by her appearance or by the calm, effortless aura she brought with her, as if she were the embodiment of a perfect summer day.

"I'm Eve."

Chapter 18: Eve
They're back

Bits and pieces of past memories came rushing back to Eve—the doctors said it would happen. Images of him came rushing through her, making her stop, flushed.

Clay.

The warm feeling of safety spread in her chest, her arms, her stomach. The feeling of his presence, his existence in her memory. His eyes, his shoulders, his hands on her. *How could I possibly forget? My Clay.*

The man who had interrupted her streak of sadness. The man who had charmed his way into her heart. The man who had brought her pure relief. Relief that she may have chosen the right path, that she may have moved for a reason. The reason she was even doing the art show…she sucked in her breath. *Wait. Where was he?*

She started shuffling along then, hoping the movement would keep jogging her memory. The hallway was dim, stirrings from the nearby rooms came as she passed, slowly, very slowly.

A noise stopped her. *Thud. Thud. Thud.*

The hairs on her neck stood up then, and she stopped. *What was that?* She looked back. Empty hall. *It's a hospital, there are other people here.*

She kept going, heading back to her room. Her mind went back to Clay and this newfound information.

Was he safe? Was he alive?

Just the thought of him possibly dead made her well up. Anger started to build in her chest.

She was suddenly struck by thoughts of him, she recalled his way, his demeanor, everything about him. She had fallen hard, fast, and she knew it. She hadn't been able to help herself. That was the truth. It was the only time in her life where she truly let go, and allowed herself to have the thing she wanted. Him. And she took it.

She knew that she shouldn't be careless. She knew. And now, she was in deep. *And he was too.*

Her hands moved to her stomach. She looked down, confused.

She was so frustrated that she didn't have her phone, didn't have contact with the outside world, to Clay. She had to get out of here.

She had to find out what happened to him—to everything. Taking a deep breath, she decided it was time to go. She couldn't wait until morning, she needed answers. Now.

Where would I go? She couldn't go home with this maniac still out there. She couldn't go back to the studio.

Thud. Thud. *Thud.*

There it was again. And it was coming from her room. She stopped, held her breath. *The night nurse, probably.*

Eve inched closer to the door, trying not to make noise with her stupid crutch. A loud crash made her stop outside the door short.

There was a shadow in the dark, against the darkness, hunched over the empty bed. The crashing sound happened again and Eve jerked back.

Oh no, no, no.

Eve leaned in and her eyes went wide. This was definitely not the night nurse in the friendly scrubs. This was not the doctor in the white coat. This was a stranger, in all black. *They're back.*

She slowly turned and rolled along the wall to the right, sliding her body until she was almost to the neighboring doorway. She kept her eyes on the room the entire time she inched backward. Pain emanated from her foot.

Finding the door next to hers, she slowly turned the knob, and breathed out a sigh of relief as she slid her body inside, leaving just a crack in the doorway. She watched and waited.

They're back for me.

Chapter 19: Clay
It's part of the gig

Clay's smile froze on his face, and he snapped back into reality before making it extremely awkward.

"Hi, yes!" he said a little too loudly, widening the door. He was still squinting against the warm Florida sun, but he saw her. "Come in, come in. I'm Clay."

Eve Brooks was a total knockout for lack of a better term. Literally, a gorgeous specimen of a thing, with just about every feature of old school beauty. She had long flowing locks of blonde, with tall slender curves up and down her body, and a beautiful smile. *She's a natural beauty.*

"Sorry, I was walking by when you returned my call, I know that sounds crazy, but I really was. I love Del Ray beach…" she trailed off, looking around. She slid the oversized sunglasses down her nose and revealed her big, carbon blue eyes.

Clay stood there for a moment, taking her in. He had to chuckle to himself. Two beautiful women had now entered his life.

And for years, there had been not one. He couldn't help but watch her as she slowly twirled, looking at the space around her.

He took in her flowing pale dress covering up a light blue bikini, and a full body of pure perfection. Everything she was wearing was sheer—transparent, even. There were bits of sand on her tan legs, the smell of the sea in the air. Everything about Eve screamed fun in the sun. *Wild and free.*

"Wow." Her voice softly kissed the walls. "This place."

Wow is right.

Clay lifted his gaze, aware he was staring. "I'm happy to show you around. Apologies for the bed head here." He pointed to his hair and grinned.

She smiled again, so easily.

"This is it. This is my place." He started to walk, and she followed.

"It's…amazing." And, he could tell she really meant it. She could see the magic in it, in all of it. *She gets it.*

"You came at the perfect time."

Eve's eyes followed him, not the room, as he talked and walked. He could feel her eyes on him, staring at his shoulders, his muscles under his shirt. Her eyes traveled down his body. He was telling the story of how the studio came to be. But he was enjoying her watching him.

"And then, recently I received some funding, and brought this beauty back to life," he said, as he circled his arms around widely in the space.

She smiled, looking around. "It's perfect. Where do I sign?" she asked, laughing easily. It echoed in the warehouse.

I could get used to that laugh.

He smiled too, and they stood there, lingering on each other a moment too long.

"So, you're an artist?" His voice was thick.

"Yeah, well, aspiring artist, you know how it goes. I've had a few shows, I have lots of art, and even more trauma—" she stopped short, eyeballing him.

He laughed. "It's part of the gig."

"It sure is."

They smiled at each other, and there was that moment
—each of them held it for just a bit too long.

Clay hitched his breath. *I think I'm in love.*

Chapter 20: Eve
The bed was filled with red

Still breathing heavily, Eve's heart pounded. She turned around slightly and saw a very old, very asleep, man. He was hooked up to a machine that was quite loud. His snoring was even louder.

Relieved to see she didn't have to explain herself, she waited, trying to listen out into the hall. She heard something but couldn't put her finger on it. Finally, she saw a shadowy figure emerge from her room through the slit in the door.

Taking a big breath, she ventured back out. Around the doorframe she went, and pitched herself toward her room on her crutch. Her ankle was smarting now.

The door to her room was ajar, the room was a mess. *Please be gone.*

No one was in there. The machines were unplugged, one even leaning against the bed in a haphazard mess. The small side table was turned over, the folding closets opened, empty.

Then she saw it.

The bed was filled with red. The words were written with vengeance and fury.

SHE LIES.

The red splattered wording was still wet, and it extended from the pillow to the end of the bed in huge, ugly letters. Eve's hand flew to her mouth and she gasped. She felt the familiar wrecking ball in her stomach, and her breath stopped short. The room started to tilt on it's axis. *Breathe, come on, breathe.*

Eve's first instinct was to clean it up. She stood there, leaning on her crutch, thinking. *Get rid of the evidence, get rid of everything.*

Slowly, she closed the door behind her and stepped back in, looking at the horrible scene before her. She hadn't recognize that shadowy figure at all. *Was it a woman?*

She backed up slowly toward the door, thinking crazy thoughts. *Get a photo of this, get documentation. Then just go. Get out.*

As fast as she could hobble, she slipped back into the old man's room. She made her way over to the stand beside his bed and gingerly looked down. He snored soundly. Grabbing a black cell phone off the table along with the attached charger, she backed away. *Sorry, old man.*

Taking the phone, she left the room as quietly as she could. She heard a snort behind her, but kept moving. *I hope they don't have cameras in these rooms.*

She got back into her room without interruption and tossed the crutch aside. She was already over them.

Turning the light on, she opened the phone—no passcode, thank you, old man—and took a few pictures of the bed from different angles. She even took a picture of the date on the board in front of her. *Evidence.*

It still made her shudder. *She lies. What did it mean?* But she had no time to think now. She set the phone down, and started to wrap up the bed sheets. The wetness was still seeping into the bed. She touched it, smelled it.

Paint. It's only paint.

Quickly she balled the bedding into a huge pile and shoved it in the closet, barely closing the folded doors over it. She righted the machine and the end table, carefully. She grabbed the phone, and slipped on a sweatshirt and pants Dalton had brought to her. *This will have to do.*

She opened the door and set out into the dark hall.

Chapter 21: Clay
This is not good

Clay kicked his feet up in his apartment above the studio and cracked open a cold beer.

He had just spent two hours talking to a beautiful girl who is now hosting an art show this month at his new studio. He felt a strong connection with her. He also just spent the evening with another beautiful woman who can't stop running into his arms, and who is now funding his art studio. He frowned. *This could get messy.*

He pulled his phone out and flipped through some news apps on his phone, catching up. Lyla hadn't called, no big deal, he definitely hadn't checked his phone hundreds of times that day, that was for sure. He contemplated reaching out to Lyla, then dismissed it when Eve had walked in. Eve had changed, everything.

Eve.

Just her name spread a small warmth in his stomach. *What was it about her?* She was beautiful, no doubt, but there was an alluring quality to her—almost inviting. Like she was a prize to be won.

Her story was simple. She got played in a relationship up north, she moved down, hoping to sell her art by the sea, and mend a broken heart. *It was sweet, really.*

His attention dropped to his phone, where the news was flashing, and blaring as it did. A name had caught his eye.

Thurston. He read on:

Media Murders: Power Couple Carol and Vincent Thurston Killed

June 3, 2024 | Jane Hargrave

In a chilling twist that has rocked the media industry, Carol and Vincent Thurston, co-CEOs of the influential Thurston Media Group, have been found dead in what authorities are calling a targeted murder for financial gain. The couple, known for their ruthless control over a vast network of television stations, digital platforms, and publishing outlets, were recently discovered deceased at their upscale Miami penthouse.

Initial reports suggest that the couple's deaths were the result of a violent struggle, with no signs of forced entry into the residence. Sources close to the investigation believe that the motive behind the murders was tied to their considerable fortune, which included a multi-billion-dollar media empire.

"They had everything—power, money, influence. But it seems that wasn't enough," said Detective Sarah Lemons, the lead investigator on the case. "We're looking into multiple possible suspects, including business associates, former employees, and even family members."

The Thurstons, who had faced numerous allegations of corruption and unethical practices in their business dealings, had recently been embroiled in a public scandal involving the manipulation of media content for profit and political gain. Their company's CTO, Richard Greyson, was under investigation for illegal surveillance practices and data theft, adding further layers to an already murky corporate atmosphere.

A source close to the Thurston family indicated that their extensive financial dealings may have led to conflicts with other powerful figures, fueling speculation that their wealth may have ultimately led to their tragic end.

As the investigation continues, the media world is left to grapple with the grim reality that those who controlled the flow of information may have been hiding their own darkest secrets.

For now, the questions surrounding Carol and Vincent Thurston's deaths remain unanswered—but one thing is clear: the true cost of their power may have been more than anyone could have imagined.

Clay stopped reading and his phone tipped back as he stared off. *Lyla's parents…were corrupt?* Processing this, his mind went back to their conversations. His heart skipped as he thought of his connection with her. This studio. *Could it be funded with blood money?*

A text came through and vibrated in his hand, startling him. The beer slipped and he almost dropped it, catching it just in time.

It was Lyla.

It read: **Hey, had to get to an early morning—thank you for last night. I'll be in touch.**

He read it, and read it again. *Did she just thank me for sleeping with her?*

Sitting there, perplexed, he drank his now-foamy beer. He didn't respond. This was too much.

He shifted in his seat and continued researching any news on her parents. More of the same, but he had a horrible feeling in his stomach.

This is not good.

Chapter 22: Eve
They're still after me

Eve raised her hand to knock on the door, aware that it was just breaking dawn. The sun hadn't even cracked the sky.

It was humid already as she stood there, waving to the Uber driver. She silently thanked Dalton for giving her some cash. She really felt awful, out of place, alone. No purse, no wallet, a stolen phone—she was in the wild. Injured, and alone.

He's not going to answer.

Finally, the lock slowly turned and the door creaked open a bit. Then a bit more. Dalton peered out, his eyes squinted and sleepy.

"Evie?" he asked, his voice groggy.

She attempted a smile. *I hate when you call me that.* "I had nowhere else to go."

He opened the door wider, an invitation. He was wearing nothing but briefs and slippers. *Tight briefs.*

Eve shuffled in, banging her crutch against the door. "Sorry." She moved past him, awkwardly. He said nothing and walked slowly past her to the kitchen. She followed.

I shouldn't be here.

Looking around, she saw that his place was plain. No art on the walls, no decor, no woman's touch. Dalton was always a straight up guy, pure policeman running in his blood. Get up, help people, go to bed.

"They let you out early?" He was already making coffee, rubbing his eyes.

She positioned herself on the barstool by the island, setting her crutch down carefully. "Somebody tried to kill me again, I think."

He paused and turned to her, the coffee filter falling from his fingers. "Kill you? At the hospital?"

"There was someone who came into my room. Look, they left this." She fished the stolen phone from her pocket. Opening the photos, she slid the phone over the counter toward him, and sighed.

Eyeballing first the phone then the pictures, he gave her a look. "Same as the art show."

"They're still after me."

"Do you have any idea why?"

Another sigh escaped from her lips. "No. Just that I remember the art gallery owner." Her neck flushed a bit, and she rubbed it instinctively. *Clay.*

He didn't notice. "Is your memory coming back?"

"Some."

"You left the hospital room like this?"

"Yes and no. I put it in the closet, I couldn't just leave it…"

He sighed. "Of course you tampered with the scene, making my job harder." He placed his palms on the counter and faced her.

"I didn't know what to do."

His eyes shifted. "I got your apartment landlord to make a copy of your key. It took a lot of doing, but here." He pointed to a key at the corner of the counter.

"Thank you. Really, thank you," she said, and meant it.

Home. She can go home. But suddenly home doesn't feel safe to her. Home didn't feel safe at all.

"Actually, do you care if I crash here for a bit? I… it's…nowhere feels safe."

He said nothing, finished the coffee, and finally turned around, folding his arms over his chest. "Stay as long as you need. This perp needs to be caught. Your case fell into my lap and it's bigger than you think, Evie."

She bit her lip. *I don't want to hear that.*

He softened a bit, and slowly walked over to her. Running a hand through his dark hair, he looked at her for a long moment.

"This may involve people that are dangerous." He was close to her now, running his eyes over her, assessing her injuries, and her mental state, most likely. "Are you…okay?"

"No." She felt his heat, felt his concern. And the tears started to well. She hated that she couldn't stop them from coming. She hated that she felt so horribly, that there was no ground to stand on. She hated that she was here. And that she didn't know where Clay was.

He waited. Then he softly wrapped his arms around her shoulders.

She sank into his chest, and let out small whimpers of long-awaited tears. She allowed him to just hold her, just for a moment, no words.

Dalton smelled like fresh soap even after a long nights sleep. She remembered his arms, the feel of them. She remembered how strong he felt, how safe. And, she also remembered the bruises.

She pulled away slightly, and looked up at him. "Thanks."

He dropped his arms and half-smiled at her. "It's what I do."

"Save people?"

His smile widened, his sweet spot. "Yes, ma'am. And this savior needs a shower."

He stole away, and she was left there, alone. She wiped her face, and stared down at the phone.

Where do I even start?

She would need to go home sooner or later, she had no clothes. Her plants were definitely dying. She would ask Dalton to take her to her house soon.

First, it was time to find Clay.

Chapter 23: Clay
Local, unknown

Clay let the big door slam behind him as he sauntered into the studio. He had a cup of black coffee in his hands and a croissant in his mouth. With a quick scan of the studio, he was happy to see everything in place. Once a business owner, always a business owner.

Eve said she would be by later that day to talk about the art arrangement with him, and he had been thinking about it all day. *Well, that and Lyla.*

Immediately he was struck with the idea of a security alarm system for the studio. Why hadn't he thought of that before? *All this valuable art, and all I have is a deadbolt?*

Making a mental note, he swallowed the last of his croissant and headed to the back office. His thoughts drifted to the night with Lyla when he saw the sofa, just as he'd left it. Dented, pillows astray, as if their impression was still imprinted in the cushions. Her on him, him on her.

I never even responded.

There were emails, voicemails, but none of them were exciting. He bounced back and forth between business and searching about the Thurston family murders. Until his phone buzzed in his pocket.

"Hello," he said quickly, not even looking at the number.

"Clayton Burroughs?" A woman's voice.

Clay held the phone out to see the number. Local, unknown. *Shit.* "Who's this?" he asked, shortly.

"Jane Hargrave, Palm Beach Times. Do you have a minute?"

His chest felt constricted. Jane Hargrave, he knew that name. The article. *The Thurston murders.*

"What's this about?" His voice was deeper now.

"Your relation to Lyla Thurston."

He said nothing.

She didn't even hesitate. "I won't be long—and don't worry—we're just crossing our *t*'s and dotting our *i*'s for this story. We have to cover all our bases."

He held his breath. *Shit.*

"I'm in your area later today, and will swing by for a quick quote. I saw your business hours online, just wanted to give you a heads up. Thanks, Mr. Burroughs." The phone disconnected and she was gone.

His stomach dropped. *Cover what bases?*

The phone slipped down his hand a bit, and he began breathing again. There must have been an ongoing investigation. And, of course Lyla was involved. And, that meant…

Before he could even think about what that could mean for him, he heard a knock at the front door.

Chapter 24: Eve
The finger

Dalton had grumbled when Eve asked him to take her home before heading to the station. The finger had come back from forensics and he was itching to get to the precinct.

Taking one last look around at her small apartment, she hoisted a bag of her things over her shoulder and shut the door behind her. She was grateful it hadn't been ransacked and marked with blood—and paint. *Yet.*

She hobbled down the path, crutch and bag, balancing them both, awkwardly. Dalton wasn't looking at her, he was on the phone, deep in conversation.

The finger.

Shoving her crutch and bag in the back seat of the cruiser, she hobbled in and shut the door with a gust of hot breeze.

Dalton's face was tight. He was listening intently to the call. Without a word, he put the car in gear and got on the road.

What's happening?

He said nothing at first, so she dropped her gaze.

Eve had requested a phone be overnighted to Daltons, and she had grabbed her laptop. And, she'd watered her plants. She felt 30% better. It wasn't answers, but it was something. She'd at least gotten some tools, and felt like she had some armor against whatever she needed to face. *Or whomever.*

She hadn't gotten ahold of Clay yet, but she would. As soon as her phone came back, she would be able to reach him. She couldn't bring herself to go back to the studio just yet. In fact, Dalton had said not to. Not now.

They're still out there.

She did have a flashback come to her when she was showering. A man. She remembered a particularly strange man there the night of her show. He was tall, out of place, like a corporate beacon at a hippie festival. His crisp suit screamed enterprise. She remembered him eyeing her the whole night, it made her feel uncomfortable. And he had been in Clay's face…That feeling of fuzziness crept back in to her now as she tried to remember more.

I have to tell Dalton.

Dalton interrupted her thoughts with a curt goodbye as his conversation ended. He looked upset. He still said nothing to her, just shook his head no when she eyed him.

"Thanks for taking me," she said, a meek attempt at gratitude and breaking the silence.

He drove and nodded again, but his eyes looked worried.

"I'll stay out of your way, I promise. I just want this to end."

He said nothing. His phone buzzed. He pulled the cruiser over and looked at it. Two minutes passed as he read, scrolled, and read some more. Eve's mind raced. Her stomach turned.

What the hell is it?

He cleared his throat. "They were able to ID the finger." His jaw tensed.

She waited, her heart speeding up.

"It's Clay's."

Chapter 25: Clay
I'll be in touch

A short, thin woman with bright red glasses looked around the studio with a quick glance. She had the energy of a squirrel on two cups of coffee.

"Thanks for meeting me, Mr. Burroughs," Jane Hargrave said, pushing her glasses up on her nose.

"It's Clay."

"I won't waste your time, I'm here to talk to you about Lyla Thurston. Can you tell me how you're acquainted with her?" She pulled out her phone, and started typing with both her thumbs, without even looking at him.

Shit.

Clay took a deep breath. He'd thought about what he was going to say, but nothing felt right. "I don't know Lyla very well, acquaintance is probably the best way I would describe it."

"She funded this art studio, correct?" Her eyes looked over her glasses at him.

He froze. *Is that public information?*

"Lyla *chose* to invest in this studio, that's correct," he replied, carefully.

"That's a lot of money."

"It's just business," he stated, feeling defensive. *This is what people must feel like on the stand.*

"Did you ask her for the money?"

"No. What's this all about?"

"I'm sure you read about the…passing of the Thurstons. We're just trying to get to the truth," she said, impatiently.

"And, you think I know the truth?" He couldn't help himself.

"Mr. Burroughs—Clay, I'm here to get your side of the story."

He said nothing and rubbed his chin for a minute. "Lyla invested in this art studio on her own accord. Nothing more." *A slight lie.*

She eyed him. "Do you know where Lyla is now?"

He shook his head. "No, is she missing?"

"We haven't been able to locate her, yet. Did you notice anything about her that seemed out of the ordinary to you?"

Her raging sobs. Her raging sex drive. "Not to my knowledge."

She sighed and put her phone into an oversized purse on her shoulder. She fished around in the purse for a moment, pulling out a small card. "If you hear anything about her whereabouts, here's my card. I just want to hear her side of the story."

She turned to go. Clay's voice made her pause as she reached for the the door handle. "I don't want to be a part of any of whatever this is. I'm just getting back on my feet, and I have nothing to do with the Thurston's murder."

"I'll be in touch."

Shit.

Chapter 26: Eve
Just tell him

There weren't many words spoken as Eve followed Dalton to his desk. There he found files, stacked on his chair. He grumbled, picked them up and sat down, huffily.

Eve's mind was going into overdrive. She managed a seat beside him, and set her crutch on the ground. She had no idea what to say. She rubbed her stomach, as she felt it shift slightly.

It was Clay's finger?

Dalton opened the files, running his eyes over every page, consuming the information with rapid intensity.

"Looks like they found a connection to the Thurston murders." Dalton's eyes never left the page. "Lyla. You remember Lyla, don't you?" He finally stopped and looked at her.

Lyla.

A flood of memories filled Eve. She definitely remembered Lyla Thurston. A chill rose slowly up her spine.

Eve's chest tightened as she thought back to the moment everything had shifted between her and Lyla. It had been so subtle at first, the tension simmering under the surface, until it erupted. Eve had never meant for it to happen—falling for Clay was never part of the plan. But there had been something in his laugh, the way he listened, the warmth in his touch that slowly, quietly pulled her in. Eve hadn't known anything about Clay and Lyla. And then, every glance from Lyla felt like a blade, every silence thick with unspoken accusations.

The word unhinged came to Eve's mind. Lyla was hiding her unhinged-ness from the world, but it was there. Eve had the unfortunate circumstance of seeing her actually unhinge before her. Lyla, Dalton's fiancé. That Lyla. *Lyla hated me. With good reason.*

Dalton's eyebrows went up. "Of course you know Lyla, because of Clay…the studio." He made it sound like everyone knew. Like they were famous.

Just tell him.

"Yeah, I know her." *Just tell him.*

Dalton's eyes had resumed scanning, he was like a computer downloading information. "I mentioned this was big, we have to know all the facts, Evie."

She cringed. *Stop calling me that.*

"Yes, I knew Lyla. She didn't like me very much."

Dalton waited.

"I don't really think it was personal, she seemed pretty harmless. At least I think she was. She was just…jealous." She tried to use simple terms.

"She's a suspect." He said it plainly, like it was a fact. "We have to interrogate her, so any information you can share would be helpful here." His tone changed to police officer, and she waited to see if any emotions surfaced.

She sighed. "Fine. Okay, Clay and I had a…thing."

"A thing?" Dalton repeated.

"Yes, we had a *thing*. It wasn't planned, it just happened. I didn't know much about him, it was completely out of character for me—it just happened. And, I know now, or at least the night of my show, that he was…involved. With Lyla." She stopped, not sure if she should go on.

Dalton's right hand had made a small fist, but he kept his cool. "So, this guy had a thing with Lyla *and* you? And how deep did this *thing* go?"

Eve sighed. *Don't do this, Dalton.*

"Does it matter? I was almost killed and Clay lost a finger. If it's Lyla, she's insane. If it's not, they're still out there," she said, hoping her diversion was working.

Dalton sat back in his chair. "Is there anything, *anything*, that you think I need to know before I find and question Lyla—or hell—try to find Clay?" He threw his hands up as if it were a free-for-all.

Just tell him.

"I was pregnant—I *am* pregnant."

Chapter 27: Clay
What did I get myself into?

Clay was still itching about the conversation he had earlier with Jane. He felt violated, like he should have had a lawyer present or something.

What did I get myself into?

He tried to set aside his worry as he headed out the door. He locked it, thinking again, that he needed to get that security system.

And, just as he slid his sunglasses on he saw her. Lyla stood a few feet away, leaning on a palm tree, twirling one strand of fine, brown hair. She wasn't smiling.

"You've been dodging your angel investor's calls, sir," she said, a playful hint in her tone.

"I don't remember getting any phone calls." Clay didn't like the feeling crawling in his bowels.

She smirked. "Semantics." She sauntered over to him. "We good, then?"

"You tell me." He walked, and she joined him in step. He felt mixed emotions. She felt like a very strong magnet, that no matter how hard he tried to separate himself, she pulled him back.

You got me into this.

"So, did they get to you yet?" Her voice was light, like she was asking about the weather report.

He looked directly at her. "Yes, they did."

Her expression changed. "It's part of the Thurston package. I should have warned you. But you're far enough out of the picture that it really shouldn't affect you. Not *really*, anyway."

"Not really, huh?"

"You have nothing to hide, Clay."

He walked, thinking. *Technically, she's right.*

"It will all blow over with the next big story. Trust me, I know." Her eyes rolled a bit, and she slowed, turning to him. "I want to make it up to you."

He diverted her last comment. "Why didn't you tell me about your parents? About…what happened to them."

She stiffened but only for a moment. "I did tell you," she said, pouting her lips and moving closer to him.

"Lyla. They were murdered, that's a big deal. There's an investigation. And you got me involved. The investment money…Not to mention that you're not…grieving."

"How sweet. You're worried about me."

He wasn't worried about her. *I want to know if my studio will be okay.*

She closed in on him then, and kissed him on the cheek softly.

He hesitated, backing away. "Where's Dalton?" he asked, but she stopped him with a firm kiss on the lips, hard and soft at the same time. She leaned into him.

"Come with me." She grabbed his hand and led him back to the studio.

He started to protest, but he followed, not wanting to make a scene outside.

Once inside the studio, Lyla quickly turned around and locked the door behind her. She cornered him and began to pull at his clothes.

"Lyla, stop."

She encircled him with her arms as she pushed and pulled them together, ripping at his clothes, kissing his neck.

"I said stop," the words escaped his lips, but every time he spoke she smothered him in more kisses.

A booming *knock knock knock* on the door behind them made them both jump, and then freeze, mid position. Lyla's eyes went wide as she pulled her strap back on her shoulder and started swiftly walking to the back. She gave him an apologetic look as she went into the office and shut the door behind her.

He watched her go, incredulously, as the knock pounded again. *You've got to be kidding me.*

"Mr. Burroughs. Open up. It's the Palm Beach Police Department."

Chapter 28: Eve
No longer in service

Dalton stared at Eve blankly for, what felt like, an eternity.

Slowly, he started nodding his head, resigned. He looked down, and closed the case file. Grabbing his jacket off the chair behind him, he swiveled away from her, knowing she wouldn't be able to keep up if he moved fast.

"I need to get some air."

She sat there, deflated. She looked down at her stomach. At the baby. *You tried to tell me.*

All those times she had reached for her stomach, all those times she felt something inside her. She hadn't processed it until now. The hospital reports had confirmed, even though she had never requested a pregnancy test. Standard procedure, they said. She was early on but she felt the tiny pressure. *I pray you're okay in there.* The doctors said that everything checked out, the baby would make it. They said she'd had quite a fall, and was very lucky.

Had she fallen?

She still didn't have all the pieces.

As if on queue, her stomach rumbled. And Eve allowed herself one minute of hope. One minute of pure hope that this baby would make it out of this mess.

She ambled to an empty conference room, where she waited for Dalton. She opened her laptop and put her feet up. The pain had gotten worse from doing so much.

*   *   *

An hour slipped by, and Eve's head popped up. She had been researching Lyla. She'd learned that the Thurstons were in deep. Double homicide with corruption, coverups, and an unhinged daughter. Lyla. She stopped reading when she heard footsteps. Heavy footsteps.

He's back.

Dalton waltzed into the conference room with two men and a tall woman at his heels. He was going over the details of the case with the team, assigning roles, and pointing his finger importantly at people. He was also avoiding Eve's gaze.

She flinched, in pain.

Resting and healing weren't all that easy in a police station. And her stomach never stopped shifting and flipping over. She needed food.

"We need to find any connections to the Thurston family. I mean everyone—gardeners, teachers, maids, postmen—everyone. Detective Lemons, you're up first—question them, get answers, and get it done." Dalton said, waiving his hands in dismissal. Everyone snapped into action, on queue.

Eve eyed Dalton. He left without saying a word. *Real mature.*

Her mind moved to Clay. She couldn't remember his phone number by heart. She tapped her fingers on the keys. But, the art studio number would be listed online. Her fingers went flying over the keyboard.

Results showed one local number. *The studio line. Could it be Clay's cell number?*

She punched it in and waited. Her ear to the phone, she looked around, making sure she was out of earshot of Dalton. The phone rang and rang.

Nothing. No voicemail, just an automated response that said, '*This number is no longer in service*'. Her heart dropped a beat.

Did they get to him too?

Chapter 29: Clay
I have nothing to hide

Clay froze at the sound of the knock, his heart slamming in his chest. The police. Maybe it was a mistake, just routine police work. But the chill in his gut told him otherwise. He could feel his pulse quicken, his mind racing through a hundred possible scenarios. *Had they connected him to the murder of Lyla's parents?*

He ran through the details in his head—and all the ways he could be held accountable. There was no way to explain his connection to her without sounding suspicious. His breath caught in his throat, and the weight of what could be coming pressed down on him like a vise.

"I have nothing to hide," he whispered softly to himself.

When he opened the front door, standing on the other side was a woman dressed in plain, no-nonsense attire —dark slacks, a crisp white blouse, and a badge clipped to her belt. She was mid-thirties, with a stern face framed by short, dark hair that barely brushed her collar. Her posture suggested a level of authority that made the hairs on the back of Clay's neck stand at attention.

"Mr. Burroughs?" Her voice was firm but not unkind. "Clayton Burroughs?"

"Yes?" He gave a short nod, keeping his voice neutral, though his stomach churned at the sight of her. "Can I help you?"

She didn't waste any time. "Detective Sarah Lemons, Palm Beach Police Department." She pointed to her badge on her hip and glanced over her shoulder for a moment, as if checking something in the distance, then focused back on him. "I need to speak with both you and Miss Thurston regarding the ongoing investigation into the murder of Vincent and Carol Thurston."

How does she know Lyla's here?

The air seemed to freeze, as if time itself had decided to hold its breath. Clay opened the door wider, stepping aside to let her in. "Come in."

Detective Lemons entered the studio with deliberate steps, her eyes taking in the space with the efficiency of someone used to scanning for clues. The room was a hodgepodge of unfinished projects—half-painted portraits, rusted tools, and towering sculptures wrapped in plastic. The kind of place where a creative mind could feel at home. She didn't look impressed.

"Miss Thurston is here, yes?" she asked, glancing around.

"She's in the back," Clay replied. *No point in lying now.* He motioned toward the far corner of the studio, where Lyla was hiding in the office. "I'll let her know you're here."

I have nothing to hide. He wanted to shout it—to tell the cop everything. He wanted to ask her to take Lyla away in cuffs. He wanted to ask her to keep Lyla away from him, from this studio. From Eve.

He walked toward the office, his steps slow, trying to piece together what was happening. His mind was reeling. And at that moment, he hated Lyla. He would have rather found the money another way, any other way, than be involved with this. With her.

He hesitated before he reached the office door.

Hadn't Lyla contacted the police on the day of her parent's murder? Why would they come here, now?

"Lyla," he called, his voice tinged with fear. "Detective Sarah Lemons is here to see you."

Nothing. Clay's mind reeled. "Lyla, come out. She's here to talk to you."

He eyed Detective Lemons as she shifted on her feet, hands on hips.

Silence.

A few moments later, Lyla emerged.

Chapter 30: Eve
She remembered

Dalton and Eve were in the cruiser again. This time, they were following the squad to Eve's apartment. The directive was to plant cameras there to bait any perpetrators that may try to break in and catch them in the act. There would be 24/7 surveillance and a team on call to capture and seize. *Dalton's words, not mine. At least he'd spoken to me.*

Eve felt nauseous, this was all too much for her. Things seemed to be falling further and further away from her, from the truth. She pushed worry from her mind. About finding out who was behind this. *About Clay. About the baby.*

"Thank you for doing this." She didn't look over at him. Silence. "And, I know this is complicated. Lyla was your fiancé, Clay was with her…and me. I get it. You're angry." *Awkward.*

Dalton kept his eyes on the road, a steel look behind them. She couldn't tell if he was concentrating, angry, or just doing his job. His expression was hard to read.

"Did you reach Clay?" he asked after a few moments.

"No. Did you reach Lyla?" She hadn't planned on it coming out as snappy as it did, but she was hungry, in pain, and confused.

He eyed her. "No. One more day and she'll be declared a missing person." His eyes went back to the road.

Eve blinked rapidly, digesting what he just said. *A missing person?* "Could someone else be behind this besides her?"

The cruiser pulled to a stop and she looked up at her apartment building. It didn't even feel like home anymore.

"Wait here," he said, slamming the door behind him.

Eve sighed as the warm air hit her face. She watched as the men dispersed. The crew worked fast, in and out of the van, in and out of the apartment.

Suddenly, Eve got a flash. A memory. That night. Her apartment. Lyla had come to her apartment. Flashes, like trying to hold on to the remnants of a dream. *She threatened me.*

Lyla's words blazed into her mind, so strong, Eve could feel her breath hot, in her face. *I want you out of Clay's life.* Lyla had pushed her against the doorway, had bared her teeth at her, a look in her eye that had terrified her.

Eve had done nothing, said nothing, just stared back. She remembered wanting to say something, anything.

But she hadn't. Fear had taken over, she hadn't wanted to rock the boat before her show. So, she said nothing to Lyla in that moment. Lyla had left with one final threat.

If you don't, I'll find a way to make you leave.

Chapter 31: Clay
You're not pinning this on me

Clay watched as Lyla collected herself, putting on a mask of calm even though he could feel the undercurrent of dread in the air. She was composed, in control, but this—this could unhinge her. She straightened her blouse as if she needed to reassert her authority over her own body.

"Yes, detective," she said, her voice steady, tight.

They walked together to the front of the studio, where Detective Lemons was standing by the door, arms crossed. She was giving nothing away, but the look in her eyes—sharp, calculating—was all business.

Clay eyed Lyla. Her pupils looked dilated. *Please don't say we slept together.*

Lemons glanced between them, her gaze lingering on Lyla for a moment longer than Clay would have liked. "Miss Thurston, Mr. Burroughs," she said, her voice clipped. "I'm investigating the murder of Vincent and Carol Thurston. Miss Thurston, I'm sorry for your loss. As I'm sure you're both aware, there has been some information uncovered that has opened the investigation in their death. There are a number of questions I need answered."

Lyla folded her arms over her chest and gave a tight smile, but it didn't reach her eyes. "I've already spoken to the authorities. What more do you need from me?"

Detective Lemons stepped forward slightly, her gaze unwavering. "You both have been named in connection to the case. We have evidence that suggests you had ongoing contact with Mr. and Mrs. Thurston, especially in the weeks leading up to their death."

Clay felt his stomach tighten. The room seemed to grow smaller, the air thicker. *This is not good.*

Lyla's jaw tightened, but she didn't flinch. "They're my parents, it's normal to contact them."

The detective's gaze never wavered. "That's what we're here to find out. What about? We know there were meetings—private ones. And we know there are some things Mr. Thurston was involved with that didn't quite add up. You both are connected to his business dealings. His personal life. And now, with him dead, we need to understand why."

Clay's heart pounded, but he kept his voice even. "Detective, you've got to be mistaken. Lyla and I—we just met. I had nothing to do with his business. And I certainly didn't have anything to do with his death." *You're not pinning this on me.*

Lemons studied him for a moment, then turned her gaze back to Lyla. "And what about you, Miss Thurston? You were his daughter, his confidant. You inherited quite a bit of money. What were you really doing in those final weeks?"

Lyla met the detective's stare, her voice calm but unwavering. "You think I killed my own parents?" she asked, the question hanging in the air like a dare.

Detective Lemons didn't flinch. "I think we're all looking for answers. And if you want to help clear this up, Miss Thurston, you'll have to be honest with me. Both of you will. Let's talk at the station." Lemons nodded towards Clay.

The weight of her words settled between them like a boulder, and for a moment, no one spoke. The silence was thick, charged with more questions without answers.

Clay took a deep breath. *This is not good at all.*

Chapter 32: Eve
He's obsessed

The cruiser door slammed shut, harshly pulling Eve back to reality. She snapped to. Dalton looked the same—tense, annoyed. She was getting sick of trying to read him.

She pushed her irritation away. *I need to tell him everything.*

Dalton looked at her, just as she was about to tell him about Lyla, Clay, everything.

"We found this." He tossed a plastic bag with a small journal inside it into her lap.

She looked down at it, slowly. On the cover of the journal was a cursive *E*, engraved into the leather, it was gold and loopy. Her breath caught in her throat. *This isn't mine.* She turned it over in the bag and on the back, she read out loud, "From the desk of Eve Brooks."

Dalton started the car. "Talk."

She took a sharp breath in. "Dalton, this isn't mine. I've never seen this before in my life." She gulped. "Did you read any of it?"

"In the five minutes we were in there setting up the cameras? No." He drove on, facing straight ahead.

She held the plastic bag up. "I swear, this is the first I'm ever seeing this. Am I allowed to touch it?"

Dalton hesitated, reading her face, looking for truth. When he was satisfied, he reached next to his seat and pulled out two blue gloves from a box shoved in the side door. "Put these on." He tossed them in her lap.

"Dalton, I have no idea what this is. If you think I had anything to do with this…" she trailed off. Putting the gloves on, she eyed him.

"You're saying that someone unlocked and opened your apartment, placed that diary there, and then left and locked it up tight?" he said, with a slight hint of asshole in his voice.

"Yes, that's exactly what I'm saying." *Screw you, Dalton. This isn't mine.*

Eve said nothing, and opened the journal. She began to read:

She teases

I don't even know where to start. My mind feels like it's been turned upside down the past few weeks. I met Richard at a charity function. Raising money for the local artists.

It started with a few glances his way. I added smiles and eye contact to every encounter. It wasn't long before I had him in my trap. And then—the fling. I knew I could get what I wanted if I just allowed him a taste, and I'll admit it. I was curious. And that night, Richard was there—staring at me. He waited for me to come to him. I beckoned to him, let him get close, then I told him to take me to his office, at the Thurston manor, which of course he said yes. I must say, I'm quite good at this.

I teased him—silly ideas, like we should do it on their desk. I drugged him, just a bit, and forced him to tell me the passwords to the Thurston's accounts—all of them. Poor guy didn't even realize we didn't actually do it. He was left naked, handcuffed to his bosses desk, for God's sake.

That was weeks ago. Now, he won't leave me alone.

And ever since, he's been... relentless. I thought maybe it would be a one-time thing. A "blip" on the radar. But Richard? He doesn't know how to walk away. He won't leave me alone.

At first, it was subtle. A text here, a "quick check-in" at the office there. But now? Now it's every day. Multiple times a day. He calls. He sends me messages on every single platform we both use. Not about work —no, it's not about the job anymore. It's all personal. Every single one of his messages is about us.

He's obsessed. Maybe it's some twisted power play, and he doesn't know how to let go. But whatever it is, it's too much.

Last week, he showed up at my place. Just knocked on the door like it was normal, like we hadn't crossed some line. I didn't answer, but he just stood there, lingering. The next morning, he sent me this long message about how he couldn't stop thinking about me, how the "connection" we had was something he couldn't ignore.

Come on. Connection? He just can't handle the fact that I got all the intel I need to take down the Thurston family.

Chapter 33: Clay
You know exactly who he is

Clay and Lyla sat in the small room at the precinct. It was a classic police station scene—harsh lights, uncomfortable steel chairs, dirty floors, heavy doors. Lyla seemed bored, sniffing and wiping at her nose every second.

Clay had not said a word on the way over. He waited while Detective Lemons walked in, sat down and organized a file in front of her, slowly. She was taking her time, gauging their reactions.

"Let's begin with you, Lyla. Where were you the night of June 3rd?" she asked, pencil in hand.

"I've already made my statement. I was at home."

"Your parent's home," Lemons corrected. "Can someone confirm this?"

"Don't you have these files?" Lyla leaned forward, annoyed.

"Yes, we do, I'm confirming your statement." Lemon's voice was terse.

Lyla sighed. "Officer Dalton Price, my fiancé, already took my statement. I don't have to answer these questions. Ask my lawyer."

"I see." Lemons scratched a note down in the file. "And you, Mr. Burroughs?"

He wasn't prepared for this. "No clue. What was the date? I was probably at my art studio or my apartment, which is right above the studio. I'm always at either."

She didn't waste time answering him. "And can anyone confirm this?" The pencil was flying.

"Not…really."

"Not really?" She waited.

"I don't know, honestly. I'll have to look." He took his phone out, but Lemons held up her hand. He froze.

"Lyla, what is your relationship with Richard Greyson?" The pencil hovered, poised.

"Who?" Lyla asked. Her eyes shifted and her hands dropped into her lap.

Lemons held her gaze.

"Mr. Richard Greyson, CTO of Thurston Media Group. I believe you know exactly who he is."

Clay looked at Lyla's face. It was flushed red.

Who the hell is Richard Greyson?

Chapter 34: Eve
Her eyes couldn't stop reading

Eve sat back. *This is insane. This has to be Lyla. She's trying to frame me.*

She didn't want to stop reading, but the car had stopped. And, Dalton was saying her name.

"Evie." He was waving his hands in her face, slowly. "What is it?" His face turned to concern.

She blinked and turned to him. "This isn't mine." Eve said, again. "Someone is framing me."

"It was at *your* apartment," he said bluntly. He got out of the car, expecting her to follow.

She shuffled after him, crutch in one hand, the journal in another. Her mind was reeling. *How do I tell him this was Lyla?*

Dalton swung the doors open for her and she entered the precinct. All eyes were on them from every corner of the room. He made his way to his desk and sat down, heavily. The chair squealed in response.

"Like I said, never seen this before, and obviously it was planted. You know stuff like this happens. You're a cop, you must." It felt like Dalton was half listening. Eve sighed. *You don't believe me.*

Dalton cleared his throat. "Here's what we know. The cameras are planted, we have eyes on them 24/7. This whole Lyla thing will play itself out if they—whoever they are—try to come back. And, for now, we have something to go on that might help us break this case. Right now, this is your top priority," he said, pointing at the journal. "We will have it dusted for prints and then go find an empty room and find out more. I have to report it in 24 hours." He wasn't even looking at her anymore. A direct order.

Minutes later she was confined to a corner office, a small desk lamp and the journal. She felt like she needed a witness, or a court reporter. The baby suddenly shifted inside of her. Her hands went to her stomach. I*'m going to figure this out—for you.*

She opened the journal, chugged water from a plastic cup, and began. Her eyes couldn't stop reading:

She rises

It's funny how easily we can control the narrative. The power.

I've spent months now studying him.

Watching Richard in the way a hawk watches its prey —patiently, but with deadly focus. The CTO, the one everyone admires and reveres for his brilliant mind and untouchable intellect.

Once I returned his call, he was mine. Fully obsessed. What was once subtle became deliberate. We both knew what we were doing, but he was not willing to admit it. Nor could he stay away. I owned him.

He'd tell me about the company's plans, about the new tech they were rolling out. I'd listen, pretend to care, nod at all the right moments. But underneath it all, I knew exactly what I was after: information. Secrets. The data that could bring him, and by extension, the whole damn Thurston company, to its knees.

And Richard... he couldn't resist me. Maybe it was my easy confidence, my soft laugh that brushed against his ear like a teasing whisper, or the way I dressed— always just revealing enough, always just restrained enough. But I knew he was weak for it, and I played him.

And he played right into my hands—it all became too easy.

I continued gathering intel—little things that slipped from his mouth when he was too relaxed, too comfortable with me. I saw how his guard dropped around me, how easily I could weave my way into his confidence. He told me things, things about the company's surveillance systems, the backdoors they had to the private lives of employees—how, if he wanted to, he could dig up dirt on anyone. How they could track calls, emails, social media, everything. How easy it was to see through people without them even knowing it.

Each little move was calculated, each word a step closer to the secret I wanted to expose. Richard is more than just a tech genius. He's a man who's used to power, to control, to getting what he wants. I knew that if I were to truly unravel him, I'd have to become the thing he couldn't resist—something he thought he could own, but never would.

So, I offered him something more. A game within a game. A game of desire, one where the stakes were much higher than a mere stolen password or leaked email. I offered him my body, in exchange for his mind.

I knew what he was doing. Watching me, tracking my every move. His company's surveillance systems were built for control, but control was a fickle thing when you didn't even realize you were being controlled. Richard was no longer in the driver's seat. I was. He had no idea how far I had gone to learn what I needed. I'd used his surveillance systems to spy on him—on his life. I learned about his ties to the Thurstons, the ways in which he'd been gathering information on them. How he'd monitored their financials, their movements, their digital footprints.

It was about power—about who had it and who didn't. And for once, Richard was no longer the one pulling the strings.

It was a delicious irony. He'd been spying on everyone, thinking he could manipulate me, thinking he could control me. And now, here I was, playing him like a finely tuned instrument. The same system he used to observe and exploit others was the very thing that would destroy him. All I had to do was pull the right strings.

The final step in the plan would come soon. I could feel it. And when it does, Richard will finally see what happens when the predator becomes the prey.

It's funny, really. It started as a game—one I never thought I'd be good at. But as I rise, inch by inch, with every whisper, every flirtation, every calculated move—I realize I'm not just playing him. I'm playing a larger game, one that no one sees coming.

The power is mine now.

Chapter 35: Clay
You must not know

Lyla's eyes met Detective Lemon's stern glare.

"Let me refresh your memory. Richard Greyson, the man recently under investigation for illegal surveillance and data theft. Ring a bell?"

Lyla shifted her hands on her waist. "Thurston Media has thousands of employees, you expect me to memorize every one?"

Detective Lemons waited. Silence.

Lyla resigned. "Yes, I knew him. He was…close to my parents," she said, clipped.

Lemon's eyebrows raised. "He was close to you, too."

Lyla said nothing, again.

Lemons continued. "Look, we know more than you think we know. We know you took many "business" lunches, on his yacht; there were many off-the books trips on the company card, you're involved in all of them. You were spotted trailblazing Europe with Mr. Greyson—there are photos, Lyla. So, cut the shit.”

Lyla sat back. Her eyes were even. “There is no law against having internal relationships within the company. If you did your research, you’d know that I’m not a part of my parent’s business. They made sure of that,” she spat, her tone heightened.

Detective Lemons looked at her quizzically. Clay shifted in his seat. He felt like he shouldn’t be here for this conversation. *How much did Lyla have to hide?*

Lyla started to say something, then stopped. The room felt tight. The light above suddenly buzzed loudly.

“Fine. Yes, I had a relationship with Rick. So what? So what if we had a fling? It was nothing.” She looked at Clay. “It was nothing, *really*.”

Clay said nothing. His face read no emotion as he stared at Lyla. *I don’t know you at all, do I?*

Lyla continued on, almost as if she couldn’t take the silence. “And before you ask, no, I had no idea about any surveillance or data thieving, or whatever you call it. I was always on the outside. They never included me on any business dealings. Ever. And besides, what I do on my spare time has nothing to do with my parent's death. I'm a grown woman."

Clay eyed both of them. *She had a point.*

Detective Lemons quietly and slowly closed the file. "You must not know."

Lyla and Clay stilled, the air heavy.

"Know what?" Lyla asked, incredulously.

"Mr. Greyson was found dead this morning, apparently a suicide."

No one said a word. Not one word.

Chapter 36: Eve
Lyla did this

Eve's ears burned hot. She could feel herself getting heated. *Lyla did this…I don't even know a Richard Greyson.*

She was trying to put the pieces in place, the dates in order, but there were no dates on these diary entries, just Lyla's wild, cursive handwriting. Which was strangely close to hers. *How did she do this?*

Dalton popped his head in the door, startling her. "How's it going?" He placed a bottle of water and a muffin down in front of her.

"Lyla did this," she said. She watched his face. "I'm sorry, I know it's not what you want to hear. But I believe she's framing me."

Dalton said nothing, his face a stone wall.

"What about on your end?" She bit into the muffin hungrily. "Thank you for this."

He cleared his throat. "Prints came up on the diary. Just yours. Still no leads on her or Clay. There is so much red tape up around Lyla and the Thurston family, we can't get anywhere. They may be keeping her away from the media. Or, she may have split. Or, she's dead," he said, emotionless.

Eve shook her head. "Of course my prints are on it, she somehow is getting all my information. She was in my apartment, she could have lifted them at any time." She paused, unsure if she should ask. "What happened with you and Lyla?"

He got a hardened look on his face, but his phone buzzed in his hand interrupting his thought. He checked it, and put up a finger. Backing away from the room, he put his phone to his ear. "Price," he said and was gone.

Convenient timing. She sighed and continued reading.

She closes the deal

The headlines are everywhere. "Thurston Media Tycoons Found Dead in Alleged Murder-Suicide." "Corporate Scandal at Thurston Group Linked to Fatal Incident." And my name isn't even a blip on their radar.

I can't even process all of it. How quickly everything turned, how the Thurstons, who were always so careful with their public image, could suddenly be reduced to the subjects of a scandal like this.

I can't escape the news, the social media posts, the lies. And the best part is Lyla Thurston will go down for it. She was never included in any of the family business dealings, they thought she was insane. They kept her in the dark and now she is the perfect fall girl.

After what I learned, there was no way I could have let the Thurston family's secrets live on. Not when they were so dangerously close to exposing everything. Including me.

I had worked meticulously, carefully, to get to this point. Richard had been my gateway. He was so easy to manipulate, so trusting. A few subtle nudges, some carefully planted doubts, and he had handed over access to the most secure files—the ones no one was ever supposed to see. It had taken days to sift through the encrypted documents, but once I found what she needed, there was no turning back. Lyla's parents had been more than just corporate players. They were gatekeepers, exposers. And as much as I had tried to convince myself it wasn't personal, that it was just business, the truth lingered. Killing them had been the only way.

But not until I took their power—their money.

This wasn't about revenge or power. It was about survival. And survival meant sacrifice—no matter who had to be left behind.

Chapter 37: Clay
A million and a half

Lyla wasted no time. She simply blinked, and said, "Suicide?"

"That's what's in the report. Of course, we're treating it as a murder-suicide until we can confirm. And, you knew nothing about this?" Detective Lemons paused.

Lyla took a deep breath in, dramatically looking at Clay. "No, I did not."

Detective Lemons turned to Clay. "And you, did you have dealings with Mr. Greyson?" Her pencil was at the ready, again.

"Never met him, nor spoke with him, no." Clay's voice was small, he was thinking. *Lyla was with Dalton and Richard? And me?*

"Greyson had high-level surveillance evidence that's considered very valuable to the case. Do you know, or can you please help point us in the right direction, as to where this might be?" Lemons looked at both of them. Back and forth. The lights buzzed.

"Not to my knowledge," Lyla spat, flatly.

Lemons looked to Clay. He put his hands up. *Don't look at me.*

"So, you aren't aware of the million and a half that Richard Greyson stole from your parents?" she asked, looking at Lyla intently.

Clay coughed suddenly, his throat closing up. *A million and a half dollars? Please tell me this isn't invested in my studio.*

"No." Lyla tapped her fingernails on the table. "Look, I think we've been patient enough, and I do have a lawyer if you want to continue the questioning, but I think this conversation is over."

Detective Lemons eye's narrowed.

"Or I can just talk to your captain myself. My family knows him personally." Lyla looked past her out the door.

Lemons puffed out a strong breath and scooped up the file, knocking it twice on the table. "I will be sure to follow up with your lawyer then. Sharon Bernstein is it?"

All three chairs squealed loudly as they got up and left, no more words.

Clay was last out, wanting more than anything to get away from this precinct as fast as possible. To get away from these people.

Who had he gotten himself involved with?

Chapter 38: Eve
We found Clay

Pages later, and Eve was starting to get scared. *Could this incriminate me? Could she get away with it?*

It was getting dark, and she could see the office slowing down, the coffee pot was low.

Dalton whizzed by the window. He looked intent, moving fast. Opening the door he said, "We found Clay. Going to pick him up now."

Eve's heart skipped, and she nodded vigorously. "You want me to come with?"

"No, no, I can get him, you stay safe. And…finish that." He pointed to the journal. "And Eve, we still need to talk."

She swallowed. *The baby. Lyla.*

Her hands moved to her stomach instinctively. She looked up and Dalton was gone. The door wheezed shut and she was all alone with the journal, again. Eve frowned a bit, she was really excited to see Clay. To see if he was okay.

She sighed, hungry. It would have to wait. She opened the journal and kept reading:

She owns him

So far, I'm in the clear. I almost didn't write tonight, but I need to get this out.

As if I didn't have enough going on, I met someone. An art gallery owner. Clay.

I didn't expect to be taken by him. But I did. He had that magnetic presence about him—older, refined, the kind of man who looked like he had lived a thousand stories behind those intense eyes. I found myself drawn to him, the same way someone might be pulled into a painting, wondering what secrets lay behind the surface.

He brought me out of my guilt, honestly. I could feel the heat between us, like an unspoken understanding. I laughed at how cliché it all was. The art gallery seduction. But it didn't feel forced. It felt like I was playing a role I never knew I could play, the confident, irresistible woman. I was in control, and I could tell Clay was trying to hold back. But I couldn't possibly hold back. Not now.

One thing led to another, and the next thing I knew, we were alone. The night blurred. His touch, his words, they left an impression deeper than I could have ever imagined. I wasn't thinking about the future then, just living in the present, and he was part of that present.

But now… now the reality is sinking in. I don't know what to feel. I didn't expect this—this consequence. But part of me wonders if it was inevitable. I've been feeling this urge for more—more than just a fleeting connection. Maybe this is my way out.

I don't know what to do next. Maybe I'll wait until I figure things out myself. I don't know if this was fate or just a consequence of one night. But I'm going to have to face it sooner or later.

Tomorrow, I'll start making sense of all of this. For now, I need to sleep—try to lay low, out of the media, out of Richard's sight. And Dalton's.

Clay doesn't know yet, but I'm putting the stolen money in the art studio.

He belongs to me now.

Chapter 39: Clay
Bits of information

Clay drove fast. *Where do I even begin?*

Lyla was silent in the front seat. He gave her a sidelong glance, begging her to start saying something. Anything. To tell him that everything would be okay.

"Lyla—"

"Stop." Her voice was deep, scary.

They drove in silence for a moment. Her hands were in her lap, turning her phone over and over.

She slowly opened her purse, and pulled a long, slender cigarette out of a box along with a thin gold lighter. She lit the cigarette and inhaled deeply.

"You *smoke*?" Clay asked, incredulously. He rolled his window down, waving at the smoke that filled the car. *I know literally nothing about this woman.*

Lyla said nothing, she just exhaled the smoke as it curled around her face. She smoked the entire cigarette, rolled her window down and flicked it out.

Finally, she spoke. "There's shit you don't want to know. I don't want you to know. So, just know that whatever you're thinking right now, just stop."

Clay drove, silent. Waiting.

"Like I said before, you have nothing to hide. This will all be handled by my lawyer," she said. Her face blank.

He watched as she pulled a small bag of white powder out of her purse. She opened it and was digging her pinky nail in the bag, when Clay snapped.

"Get that out of here!" He grabbed the small plastic bag and threw it out the window quicker than she could stop him.

She sat back, angrily. "Clay!"

They pulled up to the studio minutes later, no other words had been spoken.

Lyla angrily stepped out of the car and her phone rang. She gave him a look and answered it. Clay moved past her, hoping she would just go. He wanted her out of his life.

Inside the studio, Clay pushed the door shut behind him, and sighed out of his mouth heavily. *I have to tell her it's over. It's all over, and she has to take her money back.*

He felt for his phone. There were several messages from Eve. She was sending over details about the show, bits of information that felt like lifetimes ago. His mind went to her.

Eve.

He stopped short. There was a package sitting on the desk when he walked in. He looked around. Fear trickled in, along his spine. He went back out, looking around furiously. Scenarios were playing out in his head. *Could the delivery guy have just walked in? Did he have a key?*

He slowly shook it, put it to his ear. A small tinkle. Like metal on metal. He shook it again. *What if it was a bomb?* Too light to be a bomb. He took a deep breath and opened the package, pulling back the tape carefully. *Please don't be a bomb.*

Inside there were packing peanuts, like it had been shipped. Digging through them, he found a small box.

Time slowed as he looked down at the box in his hands. He opened it with bated breath.

Inside sat a set of keys.

Chapter 40: Eve
They were back

Eve slammed the diary shut, her face flushed. Dalton needs to know this—now. She got up, starving, and all her senses were itching.

Ambling up, she made it down to the break room, where she ate a hard, crumbly donut—not what she wanted at all. She made a mental note to bring food when she came to the precinct.

She looked up and heard Dalton's voice, along with another. *They were back.*

She shuffled off, the crutch clicking alongside her. When she reached Dalton's desk he was just sitting down. She looked at him, her eyes begging. "Where's Clay?"

He cleared his throat, sitting down. "We took him straight to the hospital."

She stiffened. *Hospital?* "Is he okay?"

"We don't know yet," was all he said.

"Can I see him?"

Dalton looked agitated. "No, not yet. I'll let you know. What did you find out?" he asked, seemingly changing the subject.

Eve hardened. "Lyla is behind this." She dropped the journal on the desk in front of him. "She's trying to pin all of this on me. And Richard Greyson. I am willing to bet she killed her parents and stole a bunch of money."

"Richard Greyson?" he asked, his jaw tightening.

She nodded. "And, we never found out about those keys I found."

He ignored that. "Well, we don't make arrests on bets." His voice was tense.

"I get that, but she's trying to say I did this? That's insane. And I have no way to deny it, other than Clay." Eve hated who she was becoming—cold, full of fear. "She was in deep with Richard Greyson, using him for access to her parent's private accounts."

Dalton eyed her, one eyebrow raised.

Eve kept going. "Do we have any idea where she is?"

"Not yet, but we may have some leads. Her phone is dead, and the only numbers I know are disconnected. I…" he trailed off.

She waited. *Does he still love her?*

"I don't know if she's still alive." Dalton looked down. "We need more answers." He tapped the journal.

Eve didn't know what to say. "I know. I'm starving." She looked around. "And, I want to see Clay."

Dalton closed his eyes slowly, then opened them and looked right at her. "Well, that's going to be hard, he was found covered in blood, and he's in a coma."

Chapter 41: Clay
To new beginnings

Lyla had ended up leaving in a tizzy, a whirlwind of words he didn't hear. He didn't want to hear anything she had to say. He didn't care right now. Clay had instinctively hid the box of keys when Lyla had come back in. He had no idea why, he just did it. He slid it into the desk drawer, snapping a picture on his phone just in case. *In case what?*

Right now, it felt like anything could happen. He had felt unnerved being at the police station for something that he had no part in. He felt betrayed that Lyla was hiding something—so many things. And he felt worried about his future. *Angel investor, my ass.*

The studio felt raw, open, too much space. The art around him sat, waiting. *I know, I know.*

All he wanted to do was find out what those keys were to and why they had been sent to him. He stopped, thinking. *Who had sent them?*

And just as he was about to open the drawer, he heard an all too familiar rap at the front door. *Eve.*

His heart lifted at the thought, and he yelled out, too eager to walk all the way out, "Come on in!"

The door opened and a bright smiling Eve walked through the door with her hands heaped in art supplies. Her sunglasses slipped down her nose as she tried to shut the door with her foot. Her smile was big. And Clay reveled in it.

A warm vibration spread though his chest. *Eve.*

Eve stood at the door, the light from the overhead bulbs catching the soft waves of her blonde hair, which framed her face in delicate, soft layers. Her features were sharp yet impossibly soft—lips that seemed perpetually on the edge of a smile. She moved with the effortless grace of someone who had never questioned her beauty. Her figure a perfect balance of curves and elegance, draped in a loose, flowing dress that hinted at the shape beneath without revealing too much. There was something about her that felt almost too perfect, like a painting that had been crafted with a careful hand, every line and shadow deliberately placed, yet still undeniably human.

"Incoming!" Her voice was cheerful and echoed along the warehouse floor. She plopped down a few things, and saw him coming out. Her smile widened.

"Hey, there." He sauntered up, tried to act cool, calm. But inside his heart was hammering. *Don't get her involved.*

Eve walked right up to him and hugged him, tightly. Clay rocked back on his heels, surprised. Women just kept surprising him this week. Then he gripped her back, leaning in. She smelled like the sea and coconuts. He held that in as long as he could. The world outside, Lyla, melted away.

Still hugging him, she said, "Thank you, just thank you. You have no idea how much I needed this." She pulled away, suddenly shy, like she'd crossed a line.

Clay laughed softly. "You don't have to thank me. And, you don't know how much I needed this, too." He was surprised at his candor, she was easy to talk to. *You have no idea.*

She grinned. "I got inspired. And, of course, my idea for the art show is big. As in the size of the pieces— they're huge. But I have no room to paint…at this magnitude. I just got the first canvas and it barely fit in my Jeep. Can I paint them here?" Her eyes were bright, lit up with excitement.

His chest lit up. "Yes, of course. There is a work area back here," he pointed, "and we can move that pile of clay, it's just…waiting for me."

She laughed. "Wait, you're Clay and clay is your medium of choice? That is perfect." She let out a beautiful laugh.

He smiled, shrugging his shoulders. Their eyes met and they held the moment. "Here are a few of my pieces."

He led her past the scattered tools and half-finished pieces, stopping in front of a series of sculptures. Each one, a delicate, powerful representation of a woman—some draped in flowing forms, others poised in motion, each frozen in the moment of being alive. His hands had shaped them with a reverence that almost felt sacred. He watched her as she studied them, his chest tightening with an unfamiliar vulnerability. "I made these a long time ago, when I was... trying to figure things out."

She traced her fingers over the curve of a figure's arm, her touch soft, thoughtful. "They're beautiful," she murmured, meeting his gaze. He almost smiled, but instead, he lingered on the silence between them, the weight of history in every piece, every curve. They were his past, his story etched in clay.

She caught his eye. "I can really use this space? That's great because this is one of my best ideas yet." She leaned in close to him, "Don't tell anyone, but I'm going to paint spirit animals. Well, animals, but spirit sounds cooler. Maybe that's what I will call the show." There was a twinkle in her eye as she looked around.

His eyes smiled. "That sounds beautiful."

He couldn't help but love how she ignited the room, how she effortlessly ignited *him*. Just the easy way about her, the careless toss of her hair. He felt enamored by her breezy mannerisms. *Eve, the artist.*

He scooped up some of her art supplies and headed to the work station with her, smiling.

And to think, she was an artist just like him. Finally, he could share the woes of artistry, the feelings that went along with it, and the ups and downs of creating art. He could really share himself with someone else. He realized he was jumping the gun, and snapped back into reality. *Settle down.*

"It's all yours. Are you getting started today?" Clay asked, hoping beyond hope she would say yes.

"If you'll have me. BUT. But, but. I brought cookies. I thought it would be a nice thank you." She pulled a small canister out of her bag, and presented them to him.

He grinned. "The hug was enough."

She reddened, but said, "Wait til you try my cookies, though." She pulled one out and handed it to him.

He took it, and then took another and handed it to her. She grinned, grabbed it, and toasted his cookie with hers. Crumbs dropped and neither one of them cared.

"To new beginnings."

"To new beginnings."

Chapter 42: Eve
Are you in there?

Eve had persuaded Dalton to let her see Clay. They had fought, like children, in the precinct. In front of everyone. Until Dalton finally threw his hands up and brought her there, huffing away like a sore loser.

She watched him go. Shaking her head, she turned and shuffled into the room where Clay lay, sleeping. *He's not sleeping, he's in a coma.*

The door closed behind her and they were all alone. She slowly made her way to him, taking in the sight. He was covered in bruises, almost the same as she had been—shards of red scrapes and gashes ran all over his neck and face. His shoulder and chest were wrapped in white gauze under his shirt. His left hand was wrapped tightly. His body was propped up a bit, and he was connected to a machine, pulsing with his shallow breath.

Eve had a sudden rush of emotion creep through her and she shuddered, letting out a small cry.

Clay.

She grabbed his free hand, it was cold, but there. Alive. She let the tears flow as she looked at his face, through the mess. *Are you in there?*

He was breathing very slowly, she could barely see his chest moving. But the monitors read steady. The slow beep meant he was in there.

"Clay, it's me." She searched his face for any recognition. "It's Eve."

Nothing.

Eve's heart sank, her fingers trembling as they brushed against the coolness of his hand. The steady beep of the machines was the only sound in the room, a reminder that he wasn't truly gone, not yet. Tears slid silently down her cheeks, falling onto his pale skin, her heart breaking with every passing second.

"I love you, Clay," she whispered, her voice thick with emotion. "I never told you enough." She closed her eyes, memories flooding her mind—the way he'd smile when he showed her a new piece, how his hands would move so effortlessly across the clay, like he was creating something from the very air around them. She remembered the afternoons in his studio, the way time seemed to stop when they were together. "Please come back to me," she begged softly, the words catching in her throat. "I can't lose you now."

She needed him by her side as she found out who did this. She needed him to understand, he needed to live. Not for her, but for his child.

Taking a deep breath, she lifted her head and looked at him. "Clay, you need to come back because you're needed here. I need you." The tears flowed and she let them. She couldn't do this alone.

"And, your baby needs you."

And that was when she felt Clay squeeze her hand.

Chapter 43: Clay
It's a date then

The days went by and Lyla didn't come back. In fact, Clay hadn't heard from Lyla at all. He hadn't attempted to reach her, and she hadn't attempted to reach him. He chalked it up to her handling her business, and if he was being honest, he was completely fine with her not being around.

The keys sat in the desk, untouched. Eve had waltzed into his life and he forgot about them completely. And so, they sat. Forgotten.

Eve.

Her name had been on his mind nonstop. Eve had been coming in to the studio every day to paint, and it slowly became part of Clay's daily routine. It was as if life was normal again, and he was just a guy who owned an art studio. *With a beautiful artist painting by my side.*

They had decided the art show would be in two weeks. Eve had already painted five massive works of art, and they were leaning against the walls, waiting to be installed. Every day, she would come, with different kinds of cookies, and they would co-exist happily together in the studio.

It was the best part of my day.

Clay loved watching her work. She would start slow, eyeballing the canvas, working it up in her mind. Then she would boldly swab the canvas with large strokes, creating beautiful backgrounds. She moved the colors with beautiful lines. And, then she would get into the details, and go up and down the ladder with grace and ease. Her body moved in line with the art. *It was breathtaking.*

Clay played music throughout the studio while she worked, pretending to be busy. She would sway and sing along like she was all by herself, just free as a bird. He admired her determination to finish one piece per day, and she stuck to it. He could feel her inspiration, and it was contagious.

Today her hair was pulled back into a low, messy ponytail, and she wore a smock filled with years of paint. Her strokes were strong, her face moving with the painting, moving with the flow of it all. She put the end of the paintbrush in her mouth, thinking.

He smiled. *I've never wanted to be a paintbrush so badly in my life.*

He was hungry. Most days, he would wait until lunch, then surprise her with different foods, making excuses like he had it at home or he just thought he would get something for them. She happily took breaks and ate with him, and their easy conversations always ended in laughter.

"Chinese?" He pulled boxes of hot food out of a big plastic bag.

Eve happily took a bite of a spring roll. "So, you're just a really great guy, huh?"

He smiled, spreading the food out in front of them. He took a bite, and shrugged.

"I mean it. You seem perfect. How are you single?" And, there it was—an open invitation.

He cleared his throat and swallowed. "I'm a widower, actually."

"I'm so sorry," she said, her hand pausing by her mouth.

"It's really not a big deal. It was years and years ago." He nodded, reassuringly. "I was just thinking the other day that she would want me to move on."

She gulped her food down. "So, you are single, then." Her face spread into a wide grin.

He laughed out loud. Really laughed. He couldn't remember the last time he had laughed like that. He settled, and cleared his throat. "Yes. And, you?"

"Oh yes, I just moved here, so getting to know people is…awkward. That's why I was so happy to meet you. Things just seem so easy with you." She bit into her food. Her eyes were on him again.

His eyes were on her too. *Is she into me?*

The minutes ticked by. The food disappeared. Clay pushed back his plate, satisfied.

"Thank you. That was the perfect fuel to get this piece finished." Eve said, and wiped her face. She began to clean up.

"I really love what you've done. It's really good stuff." *Stop saying really.*

Her chest reddened a little. "Oh, thanks, means a lot, coming from you."

"Listen, there is this thing—this *Art in the Park* thing this weekend, and I'm going to sit with a booth and peddle the studio. Would you care to join? Maybe you could share your show?" He asked, even though he hadn't even confirmed he was going yet. *Guess I'm going now.*

"Yes!" she said a little too loudly, and laughed. "Yes, of course, that would be great. For the show." Her smile was bright as she gathered her things and got up.

He returned the smile. "It's a date then." *This is really happening.*

"I can't wait."

Chapter 44: Eve
What are you keeping from me

Eve froze. She looked at Clay, at his hand, at him, at his hand. Back and forth, but felt nothing. *Had he just squeezed my hand?*

"Clay." She squeezed his hand and waited. A minute went by. She felt a muscle tense under her palm. *Clay, come on.*

"Clay, come back. You heard me, come on back. *We* need you." Her voice was rocky but she held on tight.

Nothing.

Hours went by and nothing. Eve had relinquished, eaten some vending machine food, and was seated next to his bed, the diary in her lap. She didn't even want to read it, even though she knew she had to. She took a deep breath and began to read.

She did it

And now, for the best part.

Everything is said and done. The blood has dried, the bodies are buried, and the file has officially been opened on the Thurston murders.

It was clean, it was smooth, and the best part is—I'm in the clear. Next up, the cherry on top—Lyla. I planted the seeds to pin everything on Lyla and Dalton, the happy couple. It will all fall into place as I watch her world crumble to the ground. And I will get Clay all to myself.

To be honest, she deserves it with her smug rich life, her silver spoon. She doesn't understand what it's like to be on the streets, with no money, and no one who cares about you. She will never understand.

Lyla and Richard will take the fall—the rise and fall of the Thurston family. I know all the secrets. I know every one. In fact, he may have to go too…

First, I'll force Richard to confess about the surveillance. Then I get the money from the safe deposit box. The police will put the pieces together, and Lyla will take the fall. She'll go down and Clay and I will leave. We'll hop the first flight to Costa Rica and never come back. And all will be right in the world.

Chapter 45: Clay
To us

It was dusk and the sunset shined pink and red across the sky. Eve and Clay had just finished the *Art in the Park* festival. The day had been bright and beautiful, filled with sunshine and smiling faces. To Clay it felt so normal, so civilized, that he felt like himself again.

Patrick had come to the park, had eyed him when he saw Eve. When she had turned her back, Patrick had given him two thumbs up with a gigantic grin on his face. He had laughed, and realized it was the first time he felt truly happy in a long time. And his brother approved. Maybe he should go for it.

They had sold out tickets to Eve's show, and then some. Her stack of flyers was long gone and she still had people lingering and asking more. She was positively beaming.

Clay was watching her. He couldn't help but smile. Eve turned and looked at him. "Let's get out of here. Want to get a drink?"

"More than anything. I know just the place."

The bar was two doors down from the studio. His favorite, an old pub, with the same five people, and the same old paintings on the wall. Decades of beer stuck to the floor and there was nothing but dim lighting; it was perfect.

Eve and Clay slipped into a booth and a curly haired waitress sidled over.

"Hey, Clay." The girl said with a smile, the toothpick in her mouth bobbing up and down with each word.

"Hey, Becca." He smiled back at her.

She nodded toward Eve. "Who's your girl?"

His cheeks tinted slightly. "This is Eve."

Eve smiled brightly. "Hey there. What do you have on tap?" She didn't skip a beat.

Clay chuckled. They ordered a pitcher of their finest ale and settled in.

"That was a huge success, thanks again for inviting me." Eve said, looking around. "And, this place is perfect."

He smiled. "It's my favorite."

"You're a local, they know you by name," she said as the beers and glasses were set down in front of them.

Eve rubbed her hands and looked at him. He laughed.

He poured slowly and eyed her. "You like art, beer, and the beach. Anything else?"

She eyed him, then the beer. "I want to love life again. I eventually want a beach house. I want to live on the water, wake up to the sea. I want the sun in my eyes, the sand on my feet. I want a little family to swim, and frolic and be free in the palm trees— together." She stopped, realizing she had just shared so much. "Eventually."

He nodded slowly, handing her a full glass of golden ale. "I want that for you. All of it. Sounds pretty perfect, actually."

"What about you, Clay? What do you want?"

He took a big sip of beer and looked right at her. "I want to love again. I want to share my art, my life, my passions with someone who can understand. I want a house, a beach house would be nice, but more importantly, I want a house filled with love."

He looked down, his face filling with color.

She picked it up, squaring her shoulders and raised the glass high. "To today."

He lifted his glass and and his gaze. *You're the most beautiful thing I've ever seen. To you, Eve.*

"To you."

"To us."

Chapter 46: Eve
Who are you?

Eve stopped reading. Her mind reeled. She bit her fingernail, thinking. Lyla was setting it all up. *She really thought this would work?*

When she looked up, Clay's eyes were open. She sucked her breath in. "Clay."

His eyes moved every so slightly, up, then rolled back. Eve's pulse quickened. *He's waking up.*

"Nurse!" Eve shouted behind her as she watched his eyes getting wider.

Clay moved his eyes down until they finally rested on Eve. It felt like forever, but she felt his gaze focus on her. Her face broke out in a big smile.

"Clay."

He moved his mouth slowly, but nothing came out. He slowly licked his lips. Tears began to roll down Eve's cheeks. Behind her she heard the nurse come in, her shoes squeaking on the linoleum. But all she could focus on was the steady rise and fall of his chest.

"Mr. Burroughs, are you awake?" A friendly voice in scrubs said coming up in between Eve and Clay. The beeping of machines and the soft rustle of the nurses' scrubs filled the room, as she checked his vitals.

Clay moved his head a little to the side, slowly, so slowly.

"Clay, can you hear us?" Eve asked, fear in her voice.

Clay cleared his throat and looked at the nurse, then to Eve. He nodded his head.

"It might take a while, honey. These things sometimes do, you never know." The nurse said as she checked the machines, pressing buttons."Good. You're at Palm Beach County Hospital, Mr. Burroughs. And, welcome back. I'll go get your doctor."

The nurse turned on her heel with a small smile, leaving Eve to finally face him.

"Clay." Eve's hand went up to softly touch his face. *You're back.*

Clay said nothing, focusing on her.

More tears came. Eve wept over him, leaning in. She kissed his lips softly, once, twice.

For a long moment he looked down at himself, confusion clouding his gaze. Then, as if the fog was lifted, his eyes found hers. More tears welled up in her eyes, but she smiled, relieved.

"You're back," she said softly, her heart feeling so much lighter.

His voice was raspy, barely a whisper, but it carried the weight of a thousand questions. "Who are you?"

Chapter 47: Clay
Here we go

The night slipped by and so did the beers. Two pitchers later and the volume of the entire pub seemed to have turned up. Eve had surprised Clay and kept up with him. They were glass for glass.

Clay leaned back in the booth. "Okay. Favorite artist. Art, not music."

Eve took a deep breath, considering. She smiled. "I mean, it has to be Van Gogh, doesn't it? No wait. Picasso. Monet! "

He laughed easily. "It doesn't have to be anything. It's yours." *You just keep getting more and more beautiful.*

The waitress came by then, swinging her tray. She set two shots of tequila down in front of them and smiled.

"We didn't order these," Clay said.

Eve winked at him. The waitress winked at him. Clay smiled.

"Wow."

Eve handed him his shot and raised hers. "To today, to this, to us," she said, her voice slowing. "To new beginnings."

They clinked and down it went. *Here we go.*

The music in the pub seemed to turn up even more, it was inside his ears thumping. His throat burned. He laughed as it hit his stomach. It had been a while since he had done this.

He leaned forward on his elbows. Leaning in towards her. The lights shifted, lowered. It could be in his mind. He didn't know at this point. He knew he liked being here. He liked being with her.

He wanted to tell her. He wanted to tell her how much she had calmed him, centered him. How much joy she had brought to the studio, to his life. He wanted to say how her smile made him weak. He wanted to say that he wanted to know everything about her.

And then Lyla flashed in his mind, and he blinked. I have to tell her everything. *Not now.*

Eve leaned in then, forward on her elbows. She matched his gaze. Their faces were inches apart. They stared at each other for a long moment. They both knew then, even though they had both already known. They had known since the moment they laid eyes on each other. It didn't take pitchers of beer or shots of tequila to surface this feeling. It had always been there.

Eve leaned in even further. Inches from his face, she seemed to thrum before him. Her lips were so close he could almost taste them.

"Take me to your studio."

Chapter 48: Eve
It will come back

The air left the room as Eve heard Clay's words.

She swallowed, hard. "It's me. It's Eve."

Clay stared blankly at her. He said nothing, his face troubled. He looked around, felt his body. The nurse pushed through the door then, alone.

"What happened to me?" he asked, nervously.

The nurse turned to him, and put a hand to his forehead. "Mr. Burroughs, your doctor will be right in. You sustained some injuries and have just woken up from a head trauma. We need you to take it slow. Your memories may feel fuzzy."

Clay tried to sit up and winced. "What's wrong with me?"

"You have a broken rib and a bruised sternum. You've also just had your right pinky finger sewn back on, and the nerves are damaged. You most likely won't regain feeling in that finger." She paused, waiting for him to digest this news. "You need to stay in this bed until the doctor has a chance to come by. If you can get some food in you, that would be good. I will call for it now."

The nurse gave him a look and walked out, leaving them together, in silence.

He looked down at his hand, at the bandage. It was big and bulky. His breathing was short, shallow.

Eve could tell he was in pain. *Clay, come back.*

"I'm sorry," he said.

Eve said nothing but came closer to the bed. She held back tears as she looked at him, his broken face. His broken life. *I'm going to kill Lyla for this.*

"Just take your time. It will come back."

The door opened behind her then and Dalton walked in. His shoulders were squared. He eyed Clay, then Eve, gauging the room.

"Welcome back," Dalton said to Clay, keeping his distance from the bed. From them.

Eve wiped her eyes and took a slow breath in. "He doesn't remember."

"You didn't either at first, give him time." Dalton's voice was steady, his eyes never leaving Clay's face.

"Where did you find him?" Eve asked.

Dalton hesitated. "He was in the bar near his studio, some waitress called it in."

Eve lowered her head, knowing who it was. Becca. Silently thanking her, she was brought back to their first "date". Tears came up now, and she swallowed them down. *Clay, you have to remember.*

Dalton shifted, and said, "Listen, I need that diary, I am going to have Lemons make a copy of it for the file. I will have it back to you in less than an hour."

Eve grasped the diary. *He can't read this.* "Dalton this is not mine. I will swear it to the day I die. Lyla is trying to frame me."

Dalton said nothing, and reached out for it. Eve gave him a strong look, but handed it over.

Clay was looking back and forth at them, and then down at his hand. Finally, he broke the silence and fired off his questions. "Are you a cop? Can you explain this? What happened to my finger?"

Dalton cleared his throat. "Thanks to Eve, we salvaged it. You're welcome. And, we found prints on it."

They waited.

"They belonged to Richard Greyson."

Chapter 49: Clay
Sorry to interrupt

Their bodies slammed into the closed studio door. Eve's lips smashed against Clay's, fierce and hot. They melded together as one, their kisses only stopping when moans escaped their lips.

He inhaled her. Her skin was so soft under his touch. He slid down the strap of her tank top and kissed her neck, her shoulders. She was clawing at his back, trying to pull his shirt up. She leaned her head back, moaning into the space above her. It echoed out into the studio. The darkness around them enveloped them.

"I want you," she whispered in Clay's ear, nibbling at his earlobe. She felt him, hot against her.

"I've wanted you since the moment I laid eyes on you." His voice was in her hair, on her neck. Breathy. *I want all of you, Eve.*

Eve's breath caught short as the lights suddenly went on all around them. The studio flooded before them with light. Clay's eyes flew open and he jerked back —looking around frantically.

"Sorry to interrupt." A voice drifted up from the back.

A figure leaned against the door of the office. A figure that only Clay recognized. *No.*

"Lyla," he sputtered, wiping his mouth, releasing Eve.

Lyla sauntered out from the shadows, crossing the studio like a panther in the night. Her steps echoed across the floor, and she watched as they righted themselves, their bodies, their clothes.

"Lyla, what are you *doing* here?" Clay pushed his hands through his hair, irritatingly. His vision blurred a bit.

She smiled, coyly. Her eyes moved to Eve. "Who's your friend here?"

"Eve, this is, Eve." Clay stammered. "What are you doing here?" *I really hate you right now.*

"Eve. So nice to meet you," Lyla said with a sneer, approaching them both in the light. Her eyes were calm, as she crossed her arms on her chest.

"Hello." Eve's voice was small. She quickly turned to Clay. "I'm just going to go. I'll just walk, it's close."

And before Clay could object, Eve pushed the door and was out into the night.

Clay started forward. "Eve!"

"Aw, sorry to ruin the moment," Lyla snarled.

Clay turned slowly toward her and stood, angrily breathing out. *I'm going to kill you.*

"What do you want, Lyla?"

"Oh no. You don't get to do that. You don't get to ask what I want when you're lip-locked with a slut, especially after what we've been through."

"What we've been through? You mean what you've been through. How did you even get in here?"

She ignored his question. "Which I am handling, no thanks to you. I'm gone for two days and you're on top of someone else. And, *her*?"

He sighed loudly. "It just happened."

"It just happened," she repeated, and turned slowly on her heel. "With everything that's happened. I'm shocked you would do this to us." She turned again, slowly.

"Us. There is no us, Lyla."

She snarled. "You don't even deserve the gift I gave you."

"What gift? How did you get into my studio?" he asked again.

"You mean *my* studio?" Her eyes flared.

He froze. *Shit.*

Chapter 50: Eve
Nothing else to do but wait

It had been an hour. Eve was watching Clay digest what the doctor was saying.

Clay gripped the edge of the hospital gown as the doctor's words echoed in the air, their weight sinking deeper with every syllable. "You have amnesia, Clay. A significant memory loss, likely due to trauma. We're not sure how deep, or how many years back it goes." The doctor's face was calm, measured, but there was an underlying concern in his eyes that Eve couldn't ignore. Her stomach churned, a twist of confusion and fear. *Will he ever remember me?*

"What… what kind of person am I?" Clay's voice cracked, the question hanging in the sterile room.

The doctor hesitated, a flicker of pity crossing his face. "That's something you'll have to discover again, Clay." He gave him a small smile and left them, together, alone.

Moments later, Dalton appeared in the doorway, and coughed in his hand. The awkwardness filled the room. Eve watched as Clay just stared blankly at them. Dalton handed Eve the journal and said,

"Copies have been made. I made the note about what you said about Lyla in the file."

"Who's Lyla?" Clay asked. His eyes were bleary. The eyelids were slightly drooped, like he was struggling to keep them open.

Eve breathed out then, as it hit her. He didn't remember. He really didn't remember. *How could he not remember us?*

"We're still trying to find her. Listen, let's just give it some time, and we can check in on these details in a bit," Dalton said. He stole a glance at Eve before he left.

Eve sat there, next to Clay, and they both looked exhausted. His eyes began to close involuntarily.

"Get some rest," she said, and patted his hand. "It's late. I need some too. I'll check in on you in the morning." Eve got up and shuffled to the door. She looked back and smiled at him.

"What happened to you?" he asked, eyeing the crutches.

"I will tell you everything. I promise. Just rest now."

He tried to smile back, or so she thought. *I love you, Clay.*

She meant to go far, but after grabbing a bar of some kind from the vending machine, she crashed on the sofa in the waiting room. She had to finish this diary. She sighed. *Now I have to know.*

She ripped the bar open and ate it angrily. Propping her feet up, she opened the diary to continue the saga that was pretending to be her life.

She was with him

I hate her. I can't stand the way she looks at him, like he's some kind of prize. Like she's entitled to him just because she's been around longer than I have. Who does she think she is, walking into his life, making him forget everything? I should be the one he turns to, not her. It's me he's supposed to trust, me he's supposed to lean on while he figures out who he is, what he's lost. But she—Lyla—she's trying to make herself irreplaceable. And I won't let that happen.

I know what I'm doing. I'm not blind. I see the way he looks at her, like she's the anchor he's been searching for. I can't stand it. She doesn't understand him like I do. She doesn't feel him the way I do, the way I've felt him from the first moment we met, even when he couldn't remember his own name. But she's getting too close, and I can feel it slipping—he's slipping away from me.

I won't let that happen. Not when we were supposed to have this—whatever this was—together. No one else is allowed to take him from me.

No one.

And then I find out she slept with him. Lyla. With Clay. How could she? I keep telling myself I shouldn't be surprised, that I should've known something was off between them, but I never thought she'd cross that line. And the worst part? She doesn't even seem sorry. She acts like it was nothing. Like it was just some stupid mistake. But I can't forget what she did. I can't look at her the same way. I hate her for it. I hate her for making me feel like I was never enough for Clay, for letting me believe I had something special with him when she was just waiting for her turn. I don't know how to look her in the eyes again. I don't know how to forgive her for this.

I have the perfect plan, and it starts with a little white stick.

Chapter 51: Clay
Another box

Lyla had stormed out, furious. Clay had told her that he wanted out. Out of their deal, out of her drama. He watched her go and said nothing.

All he could think about was Eve.

He had called her immediately, no answer. He sent a text, apologizing. No response. Lyla had ruined everything. Clay was pacing the studio. *I'm drunk.*

Angrily, he breathed out hard and gave up. His feet shuffled to the back office, and he fell into the sofa, rubbing his face. This would all have to wait. He was done. Furious, but done.

In his mind he was going over all the ways he could get out of the investment with Lyla. He was trying to think if he had signed paperwork, if there was an agreement. He got up and opened the desk drawer sloppily, his hands fumbling on the keys. *The keys.*

He eyed them, his focus still hazy. There were numbers engraved in each one. He read them slowly. *812642* and *812643*. They meant nothing to him.

He was turning them over in his hand when his eyes shot to the left. There was something on his desk.

He focused. There was a tiny white box with a blue bow sitting in the center of his desk. He eyed it. A box. *Another box?*

Swallowing hard, his fingers trembled as he opened the lid. It slid off easily and Clay froze. His breath caught in his throat.

No…No, no.

Inside sat a small, white pregnancy test. And, right in the center was a bold, dark blue plus sign.

Chapter 52: Eve
I tell Clay tonight

Eve woke up when the lights went on above her. The diary was in her lap, and the sofa was killing her back.

She smelled eggs. *So hungry.*

She looked up. A nurse had just placed a small plate of scrambled eggs in front of her. She smiled down at Eve, kindly.

"Noticed you'd been here a while. And, I saw your crutches, you poor thing. I thought you could use this. You're waiting on the man in room B123?" The nurses eyes were round with care.

Eve blinked at her and nodded. "Yes, thank you. That's so kind of you."

The woman smiled. "He's not up yet, I just left there. Eat something, honey." She walked away, her shoes squeaking a bit on the floor.

Eve smiled and sat up, never so happy to eat runny hospital eggs in all her life.

It was then her dream slammed back into her vision and she swallowed hard. Lyla was front and center in her dream. She was showing her where her purse was, laying out the items in front of Eve, explaining each one. They were in the studio, and everything seemed…normal. Lyla was pointing at the purse.

The purse. The keys.

Eve sat up straight. Those keys had to mean something.

She rubbed her eyes and finished her eggs. Sighing, she felt a little more awake. The journal shifted as she got up and stretched. She eyed it. This was too much. This was all just too much for her. *And the baby.* Her back ached. She stretched and groaned. Her foot ached. Everything felt just awful.

The nurse had said Clay was still sleeping, so she decided to check on him. She crutched back to the room, opened the door silently, and saw him there. Asleep, the light soft on his face. He looked so calm, so serene.

He doesn't remember.

She sat back down, and the pain eased up in her foot. She sighed softly and propped her foot up, putting a pillow behind her back. The diary sat before her.

She opened it and began to read:

She surprises

Lyla's pregnant.

It wasn't supposed to happen like this. None of it was. I was supposed to be with Clay, get the money from Richard, and be free of it all.

I don't even know where to start. My head's been spinning all day, and I'm still trying to wrap my mind around everything that happened.

Lyla's pregnant. With Clay's baby. Even more reason to take her down.

It's not even the pregnancy that's the hardest part to process—it's the timing. I just… I can't believe this is real. How did I not see it coming? Lyla and Clay… they've been so close, I never thought it could go there. But of course, it did. Of course. And the worst part? Clay was with me. He's mine.

I never thought I'd be in a situation like this. I never thought it would feel like this—like my heart's been ripped out and stomped on. How can he be with me, while Lyla's carrying his child?

I don't know what hurts more—the fact that it happened, or the fact that I'm stuck in this limbo, trying to figure out where I stand in all of this. I keep asking myself, "Does he love me? Does he love her? Does he even care that he's putting me in this position?" I can't seem to get an answer, and it's driving me crazy.

What am I supposed to do with this? I don't want to lose Clay. I don't want to lose him to someone else, especially not to Lyla. But how could I ever be okay with this? With him being the father of her child while he's still with me?

I know how to clean this up. We get the money and we leave, tonight.

Tonight. I tell Clay tonight.

Chapter 53: Clay
Are we good?

Clay woke up the next morning with the box still in his hand.

He rubbed his head. It pounded. *Ugh, tequila.*

Remembering the night, he pushed up on the sofa. Taking a deep breath, he hung his head. Eve…and Lyla.

Lyla's pregnant.

What was he going to do? He couldn't be a father. Not now. *Not with her.* He was just trying to figure out how to get away from Lyla's situation and now he would be front and center. *And Eve…*

He heard the door close softly outside in the studio as he stood with the box in his hand. He was not ready to deal with whoever it was.

"Hello?" Came a small voice across the warehouse floor.

Clay shoved the box and his feelings about it in the drawer. *With the rest of Lyla's mess.*

Eve was waiting at the front door, a small brown bag in her hand. She looked like she was scared to come in any further.

"Come in, come in." He ran a hand though his hair, conscious that he was wearing the same thing as the night before.

Eve smiled tentatively. "Are you alone?"

"Yes. I'm so, so sorry about last night." He tried to smile at her.

She smiled back. "Well, you don't have to be sorry for *all* of it. Who was she?"

"*She* is Lyla Thurston, my investor. It's all new and…" he didn't really know what to say. *And, she's messing everything up.* "We aren't together, if that's what you're thinking."

"She's kind of terrifying." She paused. "I got you this," she said then, thrusting out a brown bag.

Clay opened the bag, flashes of the box on his desk in his mind. Inside was a small wooden plaque. It was engraved in beautiful bold text reading: '*Burroughs Art Studio*'. He turned it over in his hands, and it read, 'Where the clay comes to dry'.

He had never received anything so considerate in his life. He had never received anything like it, ever, from anyone. *How could he possibly turn down the money now?*

"Eve, this is so thoughtful." He wanted to grab her, kiss her, meld into her.

"I noticed you have a spot right next to the front door there," she said, and pointed. "You deserve to call this place yours. And the fact that clay is your medium of choice…I mean, I just had to," she said, with twinkle in her eye. She held his gaze and they stood there, for a moment.

He crossed the space between them and grabbed her close. Pulling her in his arms, he hugged her tightly.

"Thank you," he whispered in her hair. He could feel her against him and his blood rushed.

They exchanged one long, meaningful kiss. They pulled back, both smiling shyly at each other.

Eve spoke first. "Also, I'm hungover, so we're going to need food. A lot of food."

He laughed and kissed her forehead. *Oh, one more thing, I'm about to have a baby with another woman.*

"Are we good? I'll tell you the whole Lyla story today, I promise. Nothing but the honest truth."

"Over food," she said again, and laughed.

"Over lots of food."

Chapter 54: Eve
Finish this thing

Eve was determined to finish the last of the diary. She made a promise to check on Clay when she was done, but it seemed like there was only one entry left, and then nothing but blank pages.

She leafed through the rest and two thin slips of paper fell out from the back pages. Eve looked down to see two printed airplane tickets to Costa Rica. One with Eve's name and one with Clay's. She sucked her breath in through her teeth.

Two one way tickets. And they were departing tomorrow night. She turned them over in her hands. The thin paper was just printed from a web browser, she could tell they weren't the actual tickets. *Wow, they look so real. She went this far?*

Eve's stomach dropped a bit. *Just keep reading, finish this thing.*

She plans

Alright, everything is in place. The keys are set to have the money in the safe deposit box. The tickets to

Costa Rica have been purchased. Tonight I leave behind the legacy of the Thurston family by taking out Lyla too.

She can't bear Clay's child, he's mine. And so I will finish cleaning up this mess and move on.

Before Eve could read on, Dalton opened the door and pointed at her, beckoning for her to come out. He had a very stern look in his eye.

In the hallway, she faced him, "What is it?"

"The team just reviewed the diary entries, Eve. What the hell?"

Great. "Dalton I told you, it's not mine."

"Can you prove it?" His voice was even.

"I-I don't know. Yes." She bit her lip. "How can I prove it?"

"They wiped it for prints and found none. None, other than yours."

Eve felt herself getting angry. *This is not happening.* "Dalton, you know me. You know I wouldn't do this. How could I even do this?" She looked down at her crutches. "And, what, stage my fall?"

Dalton wiped his hand down his chin and took a deep breath.

"Eve, you're going to need to prove this isn't yours somehow. And, you're going to need to do it before the press gets to you. Things could get really bad, and I don't know if I can protect you."

Chapter 55: Clay
You've got the touch

The next day Clay found himself sitting on the floor of the studio, immersed in clay. The music was loud and the studio vibrations were full of good energy.

Eve had just finished a beautiful painting and was sipping white wine from an oversized glass. Her pinky was up as she peered over her glass at Clay.

His hands were filled with taupe clay, and he was sculpting. She watched as he etched and carved, molded and pulled. His muscular arms flexed as he shaped a beautiful silhouette of a woman with the clay. She was coming to life before their eyes.

He smoothed an edge out and patted it with a bit of finality. "I'm done for the day. I can't possibly do anymore." He wiped his hands on a wet rag, and grabbed his beer from the side table.

"I do have to say, you've got the touch." Eve's eyes played over him.

"Me? You've got the touch. More touch than me." He waltzed over to her and plopped down beside her, staring at her work, then back at his. "We make quite the pair."

They clinked drinks and smiled, each taking a sip.

"I don't think I can wait any longer, Clay," Eve said and looked at him over her glass.

"For what?" Clay looked around, oblivious. "The show?"

She smiled. She set her glass down and slid over to him. Wrapping her toned legs around him, she looked right into his eyes. "You."

He smiled. *Say no more.*

"You know what they say about waiting."

"It's overrated." She kissed him hard, opening herself to him. He kissed her right back, pulling her in close. Their bodies fused, the dried clay and paint flaking off.

He looked into her eyes for a long deep moment. *I want you more than anything.*

"Wait." He held up a finger, and ran to check the front door. "Locked." He ran back to her and scooped her up, laughing.

With one swift move he lifted her shirt over her head and it flew across the room. She laughed and tugged at his pant buttons. Clothes went flying, and they met back in the middle, crashing back into the sensual kisses that were long awaited.

"I don't want to scare you, but I'm falling in love with you, Eve."

"Good because I'm falling for you, too. Hard"

And, there in the studio, under the lights with the music playing and the paint still drying, they melded into one.

Chapter 56: Eve
She tried to kill me

Hours later Dalton poked his head in the open doorway of room B123 and saw Eve sitting there, with the diary in her lap.

Jumping a bit, Eve looked up. "Jeez, you scared the hell out of me."

"We have a lead." Dalton didn't miss a beat. "I need you to come with me."

Eve blinked rapidly a few times, and then shook her head. "Okay, yes." Scrambling a bit, she followed him out with one look back at Clay. *I love you. Remember me. Remember us.*

"What is it?" Eve asked as she left the room and shut the door quietly.

"It's Lyla. We found her. We also found a video that may help clear your name."

Eve said nothing, her words caught in her throat, as they hurried down the hall. Her blood pounded in her ears at her name. *Lyla. The woman who used Clay.*

The woman who crippled me and made me almost lose my baby. The woman who is trying to take my entire life, my future.

She had a million questions, but she made it to the cruiser and got in, saying nothing.

She eyed Dalton. *What does this mean for him? His potential bride-to-be might be a murderer?*

Eve's eyes stayed on the road. "Where is she?"

"We pinged her at her house—her parent's house. We're going in with a team. She doesn't know we got her on lock, so just lay low until we contact you to come in."

"Wait. What?" *Come in?* Her vision blurred slightly.

"Yes, we need you to get her to come out. You are the reason this whole thing is happening, and she won't speak to me," Dalton paused, side eyeing Eve, who was now scowling at him. "Don't look at me like that, it's a long story. She won't talk to me right now, but she will talk to you."

"So, you're using me as bait?" Eve's blood continued to pound. Her eyes crossed a bit, then focused back on Dalton.

Dalton kept talking. She tried to focus on his voice.

"Just knock and ask to talk to her, tell her you need to work things out. That you're ready to make amends."

"Make amends? She tried to kill me. What's stopping her from trying again?"

He looked at her sharply. "How do you know it was her?"

"Dalton, she pushed me off a balcony and then planted a diary trying to frame me." She reached in her purse. The baby shifted. *So hungry.*

"Listen, right now, no matter what—we need to apprehend her. We will have you completely surrounded. I'm setting aside the fact that she is my fiancé, who's been missing, and won't speak to me, to do this. My job is on the line here, so just do it, okay?" His voice left no room for discussion.

Eve pressed her lips tightly. *This was not going to go well.*

"If I die going into this thing—that's on you. If anything, *anything*, happens to this baby, that's on you," she said, sitting back, crossing her arms.

"I have an entire squad at your back, Evie, I would never put you in danger. You even so much as turn weird, and they are all over her. Lyla is not ready for this, she doesn't even know we're coming." He slid a small can of mace into her hand. "Tuck this away and only bring it out in an emergency."

Eve said nothing. Dalton put a hand on her knee and squeezed. His eyes changed, and he looked at her softly.

"Thank you for doing this. All you have to do is say my name. That's it. And we will come in and get you. We're going to finish this thing."

She looked out the window, her stomach in knots.

Or it will finish me.

Chapter 57: Clay
I want you to stay here

It was two days before Eve's art show. Clay and Eve had spent every moment with each other. They couldn't keep their hands off of each other, either.

Clay had dodged calls from Lyla, kept the door locked, and had shut away the world. He knew it was wrong to not acknowledge Lyla's "gift" but he simply couldn't do it right now. He tried several times to muster up the energy to call, but every time, something stopped him.

What if it's not my baby? What if it's part of some bigger plan?

Those words circled in his mind over and over, it was almost as if he was using it as mantra.

And every time he missed a call, from Lyla or the police, there would be a knock at the door a day later. To which, he simply did not answer. He did not have the energy right now to deal with Lyla's drama. He knew it would blow up, he just knew it. But for now, he was living in *Eveland*. And he was truly happy.

Eve had just about finished her paintings and they consumed the space. The art studio was now filled with her artistic expression in every corner. The studio was being curated every minute with finishing touches, making the room look magical in all it's artistic glory.

Clay was just finishing up the books in the office for the day when Eve sauntered up, leaning in the doorway. "Cookie?" She held up a chocolate chip cookie and took a bite.

He smiled and nodded, eyeing her slender shoulders under the painted smock, her waist that pulled in around her tan thighs. She had paint all over her and she couldn't have looked better if she tried.

They had made love dozens of times in the last few days. He knew they were moving fast but he didn't care. He had felt guilty in the beginning, thinking of Lyla. But in reality, he was thinking of protecting Eve, and his future. Eve had wanted it, they both had, no doubt, but he had resisted telling her anything about Lyla and the baby—and it was getting harder by the minute.

Their kisses were like wildfire. Their touch was magnetic, there was nothing like it. Each day they grew closer and closer, and it was so naturally easy, that they both allowed every moment to be for them. It was a pull that he had never felt before.

He smiled just thinking about it. *Like right now, I want you bad.*

Eve was wiping a paint brush on her smock, watching him. He was watching her. Nobody said a thing, they just knew what the other was thinking. He sat back in his chair, a silent invitation.

"I want you to stay here. With me. All the time," he said, finally.

"Me too," she replied, her smile widening.

"But, there are some things I need to tell you."

She stopped, her smile faltering just a bit. "You're not married are you?"

He laughed a bit, and looked down. "No, I'm not married. Still a widow. There are other things…just things, I need to share with you before we move forward. And I definitely want to move forward with you."

"Okay."

Eve stepped into the office and untied her smock. Underneath there was nothing but the shortest shorts he had ever seen and a small white tank top that was ripped through and through with holes.

"I definitely want to move forward with you, too." She stepped in front of him, in between his legs and sat on the desk. She leaned forward, kissing him gently on the lips. "After."

God, I want you. It took everything in his power to put a hand on her shoulder and gently push her away.

"We should talk now."

Chapter 58: Eve
Dalton will save me

Eve's heart pounded as she knocked on the door of the Thurston home—the Thurston *manor*. The house was gigantic, an eye sore in the neighborhood, on top of a hill that loomed above the rest of the homes.

Looking around, she couldn't see Dalton, but she knew he was there. He was watching. They were all watching, waiting. She pushed the tiny ear piece further into her ear, feeling like it stuck out like a sore thumb. She moved her hair over it, subconsciously.

She turned toward the door as she heard footsteps. Deliberate steps. *Lyla.*

Eve swallowed, her throat suddenly closing up. *How am I going to do this? If this woman tried to kill me, what's stopping her now?*

Eve sucked in a breath when the door opened, and Lyla stood before her, a slow smile forming on her face. She stood there in a long, white dress. A familiar dress. Her hair was swept back, and she showcased a long diamond necklace and matching earrings.

Eve looked her up and down. *Was that my dress?*

"Lyla…before you say anything, I'm here to make amends."

Lyla looked behind Eve, out into the space behind her. The door started to shut, and Eve put her good foot in the door, making her other foot shoot pain up her leg. "Lyla, please."

The door opened again. Lyla's eyebrows raised and she looked Eve up and down. "You look terrible."

Eve fought back anger as she continued. *You did this to me.* "Can we talk?"

"Why would I want to talk to you?"

"I can help you. I know you're in it deep with your parents. I just want to help clear everyone's name."

Lyla's eyes narrowed. Before she could retort, something shifted in her eyes. And, after a long moment, the door widened and she stepped aside into the long hallway. An invitation.

Eve took a deep breath. *Dalton will save me.*

Lyla's voice floated down the hall as Eve stepped in.

"And, how do you know that my name needs clearing?"

Eve limped in and set the crutch down. They met in the kitchen, in what looked like a large open area, filled with expensive art and no one to look at it. It felt cold, lonely. No one else seemed to be around in the big expansive house.

On the counter in front of them there were files spread out. Lyla gathered them together as she walked in before Eve could glance at them.

It took a lot for Eve to speak, keep her voice even. She chose her words carefully. "You were there at my show. You must know the destruction. It's still going on. And…and I know it wasn't you." *Lies.* "With everything going on with your parents…I know that they're still out there, and they may be coming for you. They got to Clay."

Lyla stopped what she was doing and looked at Eve intently. "And, who, exactly, are *they*?" Her voice was tight.

"That's what I'm here to find out. That's what we need to find out. Together."

It's you, actually.

"Together," Lyla said, snorting. "I don't want anything to do with you. You swooped into my life, stole my new boy toy, and left without even thanking me."

"Thanking you?" Eve asked, incredulously.

"Without me, you wouldn't be rich beyond your wildest dreams."

Eve was desperately trying to think. She thought back, back to that night. *Rich?*

"You don't remember? The night of your art show you sold all of your art for hundreds of thousands of dollars. Those were *my* people, my fortune. Without me, you'd just be a shitty artist."

Eve's breath caught in her teeth. She had not remembered any of this, at all, in fact. She grabbed the edge of the counter, dizzied. *Am I hungry or is this shock?*

Lyla laughed, throwing her head back. "Oh wait, those pieces may have just a *little* bit of red paint on them." She snorted. "It's all painted lies anyway."

Eve's heart sank. *Oh, God.*

Lyla's eyes narrowed. "You know what, Eve? I'm glad you stopped by, I've been meaning to finish what I started."

And, with that, Lyla pulled out a very long, very sharp knife out of a drawer and set it on the table, calmly.

Chapter 59: Clay
I hope it's everything she wanted

Clay told Eve everything. Every single thing, down to the little white stick.

Eve had taken it well. She had nodded and said that whatever happened, they would deal with it together. It was exactly what he had wanted her to say. But he felt a pit in his stomach. *I need to deal with Lyla.*

That was two days ago, and today was the art show. The hours ticked by and the studio looked perfect.

The art studio buzzed with excitement as they put the finishing touches on the decorations for the big reveal. They had transformed the space with a rustic charm, hanging weathered wooden frames and draping burlap cloths over the tables. Eve's giant paintings—some towering over six feet tall—were propped up against the walls, their bold colors and sweeping brushstrokes commanding attention. Fancy tables, covered in lace and linen, were set up along the edges of the room, each piled high with an array of elegant hors d'oeuvres and crystal flutes filled with sparkling champagne. The room felt alive with the flickering candlelight reflecting off the glossy surfaces of the paintings. The whole studio was a perfect blend of sophistication and creative energy, ready for the evening's celebration.

The art looked perfect, some hanging, some leaning, some suspended in air, it all turned out exactly how he'd imagined. His sculpture even ended up in the front corner. It was Eve's silhouette, of course. In all her glory, sculpted to perfection.

Clay stood, admiring it. *I hope it's everything she wanted and more.*

The key turned in the front door lock—he had finally gotten that security system, and a second key for Eve —and she entered.

Light illuminated her as she walked in, wearing a perfectly long, perfectly hugging, white dress. It clung to her in all the right ways, shimmering off the lights. Her hair was swept up with a single white flower behind her ear. Her lips matched it with a tint of glittering sparkle. He had never seen anything so beautiful in all his life.

"Eve, you're a vision."

She blushed a bit, and slowly turned around. "Is it okay?"

"It's more than okay. It's perfect. You're perfect."

Eve flushed again and walked up to him, her heels clicking on the floor.

He was taken aback by everything in that moment. Every moment that led to this one. Two women enter his life, one who helped him get back on his feet, and one who swept them right out from under him.

Whatever he was going to do, he knew he wanted to do it with her. *With Eve.*

"I love you."

Eve threw her head back and laughed. She looked at him and kissed him on his cheek softly.

He stood back. "I'm serious, Eve. I love you, it's bad."

Eve stepped back on her heel. She saw his look, she felt his hand on her back. Holding her. "We've got it bad. I love you too."

"So bad."

And that was the last thing he spoke to Eve Brooks.

Chapter 60: Eve
I walked right into this

Lyla tapped the blade of the knife with her long fingernails. The sound echoed in the large kitchen.

Eve sat across from her, her hands shaking. "What are you doing?" she asked, more for Dalton's benefit than anything, but she was terrified. Eve heard a small whisper in her ear. Dalton's voice said, "Hold tight, we haven't gotten any kind of confession yet."

Eve trembled. *I walked right into this.*

"I can't just let you have what's rightfully mine, Eve. Clay and the studio are mine. I own them." Lyla's words were sharp, canned with hate.

"It was you wasn't it? All of it. And the diary?" Eve's words were shaking, the tears welling up.

"Did you like that? That was fun, actually. It was like you lived vicariously through me." Lyla sneered.

Eve closed her eyes. The baby shifted inside her. Her hands instinctively went to her belly, without thinking.

Lyla's eyes dropped to Eve's stomach. She slowly put her hands around the knife handle, finger by finger. "And, you're pregnant." The words were a statement, not a question. "Of course you are." She picked the knife up and held it there for a long moment.

Eve put her hands up. "Lyla, put the knife down. Think of Dalton." *Dalton, did you hear that?*

Lyla slowly circled the counter. "If you hadn't of come around, I wouldn't have to do this. This is all your fault. I had Clay, I had the studio, I had it all worked out. I had Richard, and Dalton, all playing out of my hands, and you…you and your pretty blonde hair just waltz in and think you can take it all."

The room began to spin around Eve. Circles of Lyla's face played in her vision.

Eve had backed up now, stumbling out of her chair, back against the wall, her foot dragging on the floor. "Lyla, wait, stop. I told you I want to help you. Dalton wants to help you." *Dalton where are you?*

Eve heard a small whisper in her ear—Dalton's voice. "We're closing in. Try to get her to confess."

Lyla spat at her. "Help me? The only thing you can do to help me is die. Get out of my life forever. And your little baby too. You think I'm going to let you *win*?"

Eve had never felt fear like this. *This woman is delusional. Win?*

Lyla closed in on Eve, her shadow looming over her. The knife rose up, up, up, until Eve couldn't even see it in her vision anymore. All she could see was Lyla. The end of her life, and Lyla.

"Dalton!" Eve screamed and Lyla stopped suddenly.

"What?" Lyla hesitated, the knife poised.

And, the next thing Eve knew, there was shattered glass as a window crashed all around them.

On the floor in a heap, breathing hard, with a small black pistol in hands, was Clay.

Chapter 61: Clay
Who is this guy?

The show went on for hours. Everything was perfect. The music, the art, the lights, the food. The doors stayed hinged open and traffic moved through. Hundreds of people came. The art sold. All of it, but one piece.

Eve whispered in Clay's ear that she was exhausted and heading upstairs to the balcony to sneak away. The crowd was not dwindling in the least and it was getting late. Her feet ached and she had champagne swirls.

Clay thought she never looked happier. He kissed her on the cheek and watched her head up, then looked around, satisfied.

That was when he saw her. *Lyla.*

He watched as she calmly walked through the crowd, weaving like a panther, her eyes zoned in on him and only him. She had a short black dress on, and bright red heels that matched bright red lips. Heads turned as she passed, but her eyes never left his.

She walked right up to him and pulled him to the side. Leaning in close, she spoke in his ear, away from the music. "You don't write, you don't call."

Clay huffed a breath, and said, "Sorry, Lyla. I've been busy." *Also, I want nothing to do with you or your baby.*

He looked off and saw a man standing close, watching them intently. Clay felt his stomach drop when he saw the hatred in his face. *Who is this guy?*

Lyla turned Clay's face to hers. "Here's what's going to happen. You're going to stop playing house with you're little slut, and come and take care of our family." She grabbed his hand and put it on her belly. He pulled away sharply, and she frowned. "Now, is that any way to treat a mother-to-be?"

"Lyla stop." Clay managed, but in his peripheral he could see the tall man advancing toward them. His tailored suit was wildly out of place. Clay didn't like it. "Lyla, not here. We can talk about this later." *Or never.*

"There's nothing to talk about. You come with me or I shut the studio down. It's pretty simple." She twirled her hair on her finger. She looked up and nodded to the man in the suit that had advanced on them.

Without any warning, a fist landed on Clay's jaw sending him stumbling back, and the crowd gasped. The music skipped, but kept going. People stared.

Clay found his footing and through his hands he shouted, "What the hell?" *Seriously, who is this guy?*

"Let's do what she says, huh?" The man said with an intense look in his eye. Lyla stepped back, allowing the two men to face each other. She wore a wicked smile as she saw the blood drip from Clay's mouth.

"Clay meet Richard. Richard, Clay."

Clay blinked. *Richard Greyson?*

Richard turned to Clay and swung his fist back to punch him again, when Clay caught it and wrenched it sideways. Richard and Clay went down, entangled together.

The two men were enraged, two fighting strangers who had never laid eyes on each other.

And Lyla slipped into the night, up the stairs.

Chapter 62: Eve
Through blood and glass

Clay slowly, ever so slowly, started to get up. Glass stuck to his face and hands. Blood trickled down his temple.

Behind him was Patrick, who had a baseball bat in his hand, creeping slowly, eye's wide.

"Eve!" Clay called out as the gun shook in his hand. "Are you okay?"

"Yes." Eve's voice cracked. Her heart soared at the sound of his voice. *He said my name.*

"Lyla, put down the knife." He waited, gesturing with the gun. "Now," he said, when she didn't move. Patrick sidled up behind him, the bat held high. His eyes were wild and his breathing was labored.

Before anybody did anything there was a deafening *BOOM* that echoed in the hallway behind them as the team of police broke down the door.

"POLICE, nobody move!" In the blink of an eye, a dozen men filed into the hallway, through the door,

Dalton leading the way. "Everybody FREEZE!" Each officer was strapped with a bullet proof vest and a very large gun. They all stopped when Dalton saw Lyla and held his hand up in a fist. He looked past her and saw Clay. He got a confused look on his face as he eyed Patrick.

Eve took a breath. *Finally.*

Lyla stood frozen, gripping the knife. She finally took a step back.

Clay held the gun steady on her. The air seemed to have been sucked out of the room, everyone just stilled.

Dalton walked in slowly, foot over foot, his feet making no sound. His gun was pointed at Lyla, and it was much bigger than Clay's. "Alright, everyone, just calm down. You're surrounded, and we just need everyone to drop their weapons." He moved closer. Closing in.

Nobody dropped their weapons.

Eve felt nothing but fear in her spine. *Dalton, be careful.*

"Dalton, so good to see you." Lyla's words dripped from her mouth.

Dalton eyed Clay and Patrick. Nobody moved.

Eve held her breath. The room spun. *What is happening?*

Clay slowly lowered his pistol onto the broken glass, and raised his hands. Patrick lowered his bat, and raised his hands as well. They both looked at Lyla, and waited. Eve waited. Dalton waited.

"Clay, what are you doing here?" Dalton's voice carried across the room, down the end of his gun. "Who is that?"

Clay shrugged. "I remembered." His eyes shot to Eve. "That's my brother."

Eve's heart flushed. She choked back tears as she heard those two words. *He remembered.* He remembered her, he remembered it all.

Eve wanted to run to Clay, to jump on him and cover him with kisses. The room held so much intensity at that moment, she thought she would die. Her heart pounded, her foot pounded, and she felt spinning waves of dizziness come and go, come and go.

Lyla turned the knife on Clay.

"Where are my keys?"

Clay opened his mouth to respond and was interrupted.

"Lyla…we found the video. Richard recorded you on the night of the murders. We know. We know everything." Dalton said, advancing slowly.

"Stop right there. I want my keys back." Lyla's voice went cold and everyone stopped. Dalton went to speak and eyed the knife, still in Lyla's hand.

Eve froze. *Shit. Shit shit shit shit.*

Lyla stilled for a minute. The whole room seemed to be in slow motion.

"I'm pregnant," Eve blurted out.

The men stopped shuffling, the air ceased to flow, and everyone turned toward her. She looked at Clay. A tear formed and fell down Eve's cheek.

Recognition registered in Clay's eyes, and he smiled. Through blood and glass, he smiled at her.

"She lies!" Lyla shrieked, her eyes wild. And in a fraction of a moment, split into a hundred moments in time, she picked up the knife and threw it directly at Eve.

Chapter 63: Clay
So far below, it was terrifying

Clay rubbed his jaw. He looked up, trying to find Eve on balcony. All he saw were curtains billowing and shadows. The music floated up and around him. Richard had gone after Lyla. No one knew where she went. *Screw that guy, screw them both.*

Sitting at the bar, Clay nursed his eye with a small bag of ice the bartender had handed him. Along with a Scotch—a double. He sipped it and eyed the crowd.

There were still dozens of people around, some came up and patted him on the back. He drank and tried to regain his composure. *It's still a party, Clay, loosen up.*

That was when he saw them. *No.*

Lyla and Eve were on the balcony. Lyla was next to her, close to her. Too close. *This can't be good.*

Clay chugged his drink and headed through the crowd. He wove between people, whom all seemed to be in his way at the same time. Frustrated, he pushed through.

Before he could even reach the top step of the stairs the screams filled the studio. He would never forget that sound.

The slow, falling scream of the woman he loved.

It rang out in the studio, echoing off the walls, off the people, off his heart. The scream shattered the air around him, shattered his ears, his skin. The music stopped as the scream filtered out across the studio. The crowd reacted instantaneously with screams of their own. And, then he heard a horrific thud and a crash.

Eve.

Herds of people scrambled for the exit. He heard glass breaking. The world tumbled down around him as he bolted to the balcony railing—which was now empty.

No, no no no no no.

His head whirled around, looking for Lyla, Eve, anyone. Swatting the curtains away, he whirled on his heel. He was alone when he looked over the edge, terrified at what he would see. His hands shook as he peered over the rail and saw not one but two bodies below. So far below, it was terrifying.

Lyla.

Lyla was on top of Eve, their bodies laying still—too still—while the crowd dispersed around them in a frenzy.

"Eve!" Clay's voice rang out. *I have to get to her.*

Then Clay watched, horrified, as Lyla slowly got up. He could see Eve's twisted limbs, and bloodied hair. It was a mesh of broken wood, glass, and bodies.

"Eve!" Clay shouted again and turned quickly around.

The butt of a very large knife landed on his skull, hard. Stars swirled in his vision as his knees weakened.

Richard.

Before Clay could compute what was happening, the knife came down on his finger in fiery white pain. He watched helplessly as his pinky rolled on to the floor and the blood followed.

"You'll never make art again." Richard's voice was deep with hatred.

The finger rolled on and on until it reached the balcony ledge and rolled right off.

Clay went down and darkness consumed him.

Chapter 64: Eve
I want to live here forever

Time didn't stop the knife. Neither did Dalton nor Clay. Or any of the men standing there. It entered Eve's body with a fierce hot slice. As soon as it did, bullets from multiple guns fired. Lyla's chest exploded.

The knife dug into Eve's skin, deep. She looked down and saw it lodged in her side. The handle stuck out, as dark blood oozed around it. And, before she could move, breathe even, she had a bright flash.

White light filled her vision. She saw a house, a white house on the beach. It was hot, sunny, and there was a dog panting at her feet, smiling up at her. She smelled cookies baking.

She looked out and saw Clay, near the water. He was running, chasing a small child, the sun behind them. She saw the waves, the birds, the sky, it was all hers. It was all theirs. She saw it all. She looked down and felt herself, seeing a big round belly, filled with life. *Another baby. Our baby.*

The white light faded and she saw the knife handle again. She saw the blood. This time it wasn't paint. It was blood. Her blood. *There was so much of it.*

She heard people screaming her name. She felt hands on her.

She let the white light in again, and followed herself to the beach. She just wanted to be at the beach. With Clay. With her family.

The house, full of life and love, echoed with the sound of their voices, their footsteps, and the soft murmur of bedtime stories. The walls held milestones—first words, first steps, the quiet joys of everyday moments. It was a dream, a future that seemed so tangible, so within reach, that she could almost taste it. In the distance, she saw Clay pulling their son onto his shoulders, twirling in the surf, and a sense of peace settled in her heart. This, she thought, was exactly where she was meant to be.

It was easier this way. She could just stay here, at the beach forever. Her mind wandered back to the water, back to safety. Back to the sun. *No more pain, no more lies.*

"Eve!"

Her name came from a distance.

She heard the waves again and sagged against the pain. *Just take me away. I want to live here forever.*

"Eve!"

The white light consumed her, and she let go. She let go of it all.

Chapter 65: Clay
The pieces shattered all around her

Clay woke up from the darkness just in time to witness the wrath that was Lyla. He was being dragged through the studio by his shoulder, and it hurt. A lot. He saw Richard above him, a looming figure in and out in the lights.

Through the haze, through the bright lights, through the unsteady gaze of his now burning eyes, he saw her.

Lyla, no.

He saw Lyla with his own hammer, destroying the art around him in a wild, ravenous rage. Piece after piece, she swung the hammer with such intensity, the canvas shattering all around her.

His eyesight crossed as he watched her grab a bucket of paint—red, deep red—and began to splatter it here, there, and everywhere she could, across every inch of art. She took more and more cans, until there was none left, leaving the room looking like a bloody massacre.

"Stop." His voice was nothing against her fury.

He watched all of this, being held, by a strong determined hand. Richard was carrying him to the door, slowly. It was as if he wanted Clay to see this. This destruction.

Eve.

Clay remembered Eve on the floor, lying there motionless and his mind cleared instantly. He yanked on the arm holding him with renewed strength, and thrust himself free from Richard's grip.

Surprised, Richard tried to grab Clay again.

Clay whipped around, his head whirling, and crashed into Richard. They ended up tumbling down together in a heap of limbs, paint getting in their clothes, their hair, everywhere. Clay's open, bloody fingerless hand held against his chest.

"You bastard!" Lyla's voice rang out. She was wild-eyed, paint splattered all over her as she crossed the room towards them.

The lights whirled and swirled and the pain kept coming for Clay. Punch after punch, the men landed painful blows, their bodies crumbling in agony.

"Richard, stop! We need him. Let's go," Lyla said, her voice was close to them now.

And, with one more deafening blow to the head, Clay went out and the room went dark.

Chapter 66: Eve and Clay
The fight for them was all over

Clay sat, watching Eve laying still in the hospital bed. Days had passed. It was all over. The fight for them was all over.

Dalton had just left. He had filled Clay in on the gritty details. He sat thinking of how it went down, his heart heavy.

Lyla had been taken out with multiple gunshots. Dalton and Clay had both shot the gun at the same time, firing though her chest and back. Her wrath had finally come to an end.

Lyla had in fact murdered her own parents. Richard went mad when he saw the recording, and then found the diary. Before taking his life, he shipped Clay the keys to Lyla's safe deposit box, another failed attempt at framing someone else. He then tried to take Eve's life but she wasn't home, so he left the diary there and put a bullet in his head.

Dalton also reported that there was enough evidence for Lyla to be charged with double homicide, assisted suicide, attempted murder, and was in fact, not pregnant. She had lost the baby due to the copious amounts of cocaine in her system.

Clay had also learned that the keys they found were to a safe deposit box that held close to two million in cash. And, after legal review, the Thurston family—what was left anyway—had donated a portion of it. A big portion. To Clay—to the *Burroughs Art Studio*. They wrote in the press release that it was in honor of him and Eve catching the person who murdered the Thurstons.

As Clay was processing everything, he had the sinking revelation that the times he had seen Lyla crying could quite possibly have been right after she murdered her own parents. *And I comforted her. She lies.*

He looked down at Eve now. *My Eve. It was all over. And Eve could be dying.*

Lyla had done so much damage, he didn't know what was left. If anything. His eyes dropped down to Eve's stomach. They were waiting on test results—waiting for her to wake up.

Wake up, Eve.

She had just completed the second surgery this week, and she was on so many machines, he felt weak looking at them. He didn't have much hope left.

The knife had missed several organs, but had done quite a bit of damage. *If she lives, it will be a miracle.*

The door swung open with a soft knock. A man wearing tiny gold glasses and a sharp white coat entered, looking official.

"Mr. Burroughs, Dr. Jensen. Checking in on our patient here. Vitals are stable, surgery went well as reported." He eyed her chart next to her bed, and looked her up and down. "She's very lucky. This baby is a miracle."

Clay blew out the air in his lungs and sat up straight. "The baby is alright? Eve will be…alright?"

"Give it time, but yes. She's a fighter." He half-smiled and left the room.

Clay grabbed Eve's hand and squeezed hard. "Eve, you're going to be okay, did you hear that?" *You're going to be okay.*

Clay closed his eyes as a tear made it's way down his cheek. And as he did, he saw them. Together. Their family, on the beach. Just swimming, playing, and being together.

He squeezed his eyes and put his hands together.

"God, if you're listening, please save her. Save my Eve."

Eve stirred. Her eyebrows raising first, then her eyelids. She said nothing.

"Eve, it's me." Clay's eyes were wide, as he watched her wake from her restless state. He went to call the nurse but stopped.

She coughed, and winced. *Where am I?*

"Eve?"

"Who are you?" Her voice was garbled, weak.

His heart sank. *She doesn't remember.*

Then, a small smile curled her lips and it rolled into an even bigger one. Clay waited, confused.

"How could I forget the father of my child?" She said then, pulling him in by the hand. *My Clay.*

Clay let out another big breath and came in fully to hug her as best he could. Tears ran down their faces as they looked at each other once more. They sat there like that for a long time, just holding each other.

"What's happened?"

He slowly filled her in on what happened. She took it all in, tears flowing down her cheeks.

He smiled. "I brought cookies." He took one out, broke it in half and handed it to her.

Through tears, she took it, and they clinked them together in a cheer. "To us."

"Oh, and will you marry me?"

Eve smiled. "Yes, of course I will marry you."

He hugged her tighter, kissing her eyelids and forehead, kissing her face everywhere he could. "And, I may or may not have purchased a house on the beach."

Eve laughed softly. "I can't wait to see it."

Tears rolled down their cheeks as they winced, still in pain. But in pain, together.

She rubbed her stomach. "What should we name her?"

"It's a girl?" he asked, his eyes brightening. "Anything but Lyla."

They both smiled. *Anything but Lyla.*

About the Author

Caylin Brie White is an Editorial Lead at *Salesforce*, a certified Mindful Meditation and Breath Leader, Human Design Coach, and the creator of *Breathe With Me, Caylin Brie* (**www.breathewithmecaylinbrie.com**). Visit Udemy to view her certifications and courses. She lives in St. Augustine, Florida with her husband and rescue pup, Sophie.

Acknowledgements

I would like to express my deepest gratitude to all those who have supported me throughout this journey.

First and foremost, I would like to thank my husband, Patrick, for his encouragement, and belief in me and my work. His insightful feedback have been instrumental in shaping this book. Not to mention his insane ability to design—thanks for creating the cover of this one, Bear.

I'm also deeply appreciative of my family, whose love and support made this process both inspiring and enjoyable. To my mom and sister, our ladies dinner conversations have helped me more than you know. Thanks for always checking in on me.

I would also like to acknowledge my friends, my soul sisters and brothers, whose patience, love, and constant encouragement have been my foundation. To all, thank you for joining me on this wild ride.

Lastly, my sincere thanks go to all those who, in one way or another, helped me on this journey. While their names may not all appear here, their contributions are greatly appreciated.

Thank you, for everything.

www.ingramcontent.com/pod-product-compliance
Lightning Source LLC
Chambersburg PA
CBHW041750310726
48978CB00011BB/386